Hugo Reid

First Book of Mathematics

being an easy and practical introduction to the study; for self-instruction

and use in schools

Hugo Reid

First Book of Mathematics
being an easy and practical introduction to the study; for self-instruction and use in schools

ISBN/EAN: 9783337387945

Printed in Europe, USA, Canada, Australia, Japan

Cover: Foto ©Andreas Hilbeck / pixelio.de

More available books at **www.hansebooks.com**

FIRST BOOK

OF

MATHEMATICS,

BEING

AN EASY AND PRACTICAL INTRODUCTION TO THE STUDY;

FOR SELF-INSTRUCTION AND USE IN SCHOOLS.

BY

HUGO REID,

LATELY PRINCIPAL OF THE DALHOUSIE COLLEGE, HALIFAX, N.S.
Author of various Educational Treatises.

EDINBURGH:
ADAM & CHARLES BLACK.
1872.

PREFACE.

—◇—

This little work, so far as I know, is new in its object and plan.

Its design is, to place a body of interesting, practical, and useful mathematical knowledge within reach of that large class in middle and elementary schools, who have not time for Euclid or any such course. The pupil can work at it mostly by himself, with occasional superintendence by the teacher ; or it may be used as a lesson book in classes. He will learn from it the nature of geometrical figures ; how to do the leading problems in practical geometry ; how to construct the leading kinds of plane figures ; to read and understand algebraic expressions, including the simpler equations ; and to solve the principal questions in mensuration, in which numerous practical exercises are given. He will thus become initiated in mathematical language and ideas ; be subjected to a valuable mental exercise ; acquire a body of useful knowledge, thorough so far as it goes ; and lay such a foundation as will make it easy for him to take up the subject afterwards, should taste or professional requirements lead him to recur to it. In occasional notes, I have pointed out interesting and important geometrical truths, illustrated by the problems.

It is much to be regretted that a large majority of the youth of this country leave school utterly unacquainted with the useful and beautiful truths of algebra and geometry. For them, save a little arithmetic, the noble sciences of the mathematics do not exist. They are sent into the world without that mental training, derived from exercise in the exact definitions, problems, rules of mathematics; without that valuable training of hand and eye, imparted by the careful construction of geometrical figures; unable to work a common question in mensuration; unable to understand a simple algebraic formula; and hence, incapable of comprehending elementary truths in important departments of science and art. They are quite deficient in that early foundation on which to rear an after structure of scientific education or technical knowledge; and, from want of a little rudimentary instruction, are unfit to rise above the lowest grades of work in the mechanical arts.

These radical defects in the education of so many of our youth are owing mainly to four causes :—

The want of a suitable text-book.

The notion that Euclid is the only possible introduction to the study of mathematics.

The time wasted on elementary arithmetic, from the want of a decimal system of money, weights, and measures.

The early age at which children are removed from school.

The present work is designed to supply a suitable text-book. A boy of twelve or thirteen years of age may go through it. He will then have some knowledge of fundamental facts and principles in mathematics; may acquire some skill in the construction of figures and in ordinary questions in mensuration, and will not find an algebraic formula altogether an unknown tongue.

I have had some experience in education, and venture to submit this work as an introduction to mathematics specially for beginners, and containing enough for that large class that leave school before fifteen years of age, who have so much to crowd into a limited time. Though not a demonstrative course, it contains much calculated to impart valuable training, to interest, to be useful, and to excite a taste for further progress. But the teacher will, doubtless, make the pupil aware that there are demonstrations—which he should study when he has time—and give him orally examples of these.

H. R.

LONDON, *February* 1872.

CONTENTS.

——◇——

FIRST BOOK OF MATHEMATICS.

———◆———

I. ELEMENTARY DEFINITIONS.

Point—Line—Plane—Circle—Angle—Parallel Lines.

1. Each page or side of this leaf is A SURFACE. It has a certain shape or *form*. It has a certain size or *magnitude*, depending on its *length* and *breadth*. It may be quite *flat*, or more or less bent—that is, *curved*.

2. The edges or boundaries of the leaf are LINES. Each line has *length*, but not breadth, or next to none. In geometry, we speak of lines as if they had no breadth, though we cannot draw any line entirely without breadth. But we may reason about them as if they had no breadth. Also, the edges of the leaf may be *straight* or *curved*.

3. But the book has more than length and breadth. It has also thickness or *depth*. In geometry, a thing that has these three properties is called a SOLID. A solid, in a geometrical sense, need not have body or substance all through. An empty room, a vessel from which the air has been taken out, or a portion of space considered by itself, are solids, speaking geometrically.

4. The boundary of a solid is a surface, or surfaces.

A

5. These three, length, breadth, and depth, are called *dimensions*.

6. The forms and dimensions of solids, surfaces, and lines are the objects of geometry.

7. The ends of the edges of the leaf and the corners of the book are POINTS. A point has neither length nor breadth—no magnitude of any kind. But it is in a certain place ; that is, it has *position;* and it is useful in geometry to refer to points, to enable us to indicate exactly particular places or positions.

Hence flow the following definitions :—

8. *A point* is that which has position, but not magnitude.

A point is named by a letter placed close to it.

9. *A line* is that which has length without breadth.

A line is named by letters placed at its ends.

The ends of a line are points, and the intersection (crossing) of one line with another is also a point.

10. A STRAIGHT LINE is a line which lies evenly between its ends; that is, which points all in one direction.

The adjoining is a straight line, called AB, as indicating the direction from A to B, or BA, denoting the opposite direction, from B to A.

FIG. I

A ————————————————————————— B

11. A straight line is the shortest way between two points. The *distance* between two points means the straight line between them. Only one straight line can be drawn between two points.

12. The word *rectilineal,* means " straight-lined."

13. A CURVED LINE, or CURVE, is a line which is continually changing its direction.

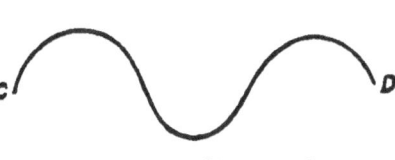

FIG. 2

CD is a curved line.

14. A SURFACE is that which has only length and breadth.

The edge or boundary of a surface is a line or lines.

15. A PLANE SURFACE, or PLANE, is a surface in which, any two points being taken, the straight line between them lies wholly in that surface; that is, every point of such straight line touches the surface.

A plane is a perfectly flat surface, as the top of a table, the board of a book, the wall or floor of a room. The surface of any liquid of moderate extent may be considered a plane, but not that of a drop, which is a curved or round surface, nor that of a large body of water, which partakes of the roundness of the earth's surface.

Every point in the straight edge of a well-made flat ruler touches a true plane, at whatever part of the plane it is laid along it.

16. There are some curved surfaces on which straight lines may be drawn, coinciding with them at every point, as a cylinder or a cone. But this cannot be done between two points *anywhere*, only at particular parts.

17. A SOLID is that which has the three dimensions, length, breadth, and depth.

18. A PLANE FIGURE is a portion of a plane surface enclosed within a line or lines. If contained by several lines, they are called its sides.

19. THE PERIMETER of a plane figure is the whole length of the line or lines which contain it.

20. THE AREA of a plane figure is the quantity or extent of surface which it contains.

The Circle.

21. A CIRCLE is a plane figure, bounded by one curved line, every point of which is at the same distance from a point within it called THE CENTRE.

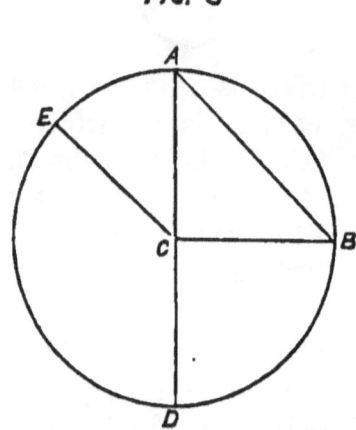

FIG. 3

The bounding line, or perimeter, is called *the circumference* of the circle.

22. The adjoining figure, EABD, is a circle; the point C is the centre, which is equidistant from every point in the circumference; that is, the straight lines CE, CA, CB, CD, and all such lines, are equal in length.

23. A RADIUS (*plural*, radii) is any straight line from the centre of a circle to the circumference; as, the lines just named.

24. All radii of the same circle are equal in length.

25. AN ARC of a circle is any part of the circumference; as, the curved lines AE, ED, DB, AB.

26. A CHORD of a circle is a straight line joining any two points of the circumference.

The straight lines AB, AD, are chords.

27. A chord is called the chord of either of the arcs whose ends it joins. AB is the chord of the large arc from A by E and D to B. It is also the chord of the small arc forming the remainder of the circumference.

28. A DIAMETER of a circle is a chord passing through its centre. AD is a diameter.

The diameter of a circle is manifestly double of its radius. The radii, CA, CD, are equal, and the diameter AD is double of either of them.

29. A SEGMENT of a circle is the part contained by any arc and its chord.

The figure AEDB is a segment; also the figure contained by the straight line AB and the small arc on the other side of it.

30. A SEMICIRCLE is a segment, the chord of which is a diameter.

AED and ABD are semicircles.

31. A SECTOR of a circle is the part enclosed by two radii, and the arc joining their ends.

CEA (or CAE) is a sector.

32. A TANGENT to a circle is a straight line which meets the circumference in only one point, all the rest of it being outside of the circle. It is said to *touch* the circle.

33. When the radius of one circle is equal to the radius of another circle, the two circles are equal in all respects; all their radii are equal; their diameters are equal; their circumferences are equal; and their areas are equal. The two circles are identical, and one could be laid upon the other, so that the two centres and the two circumferences would exactly coincide.

Division of the Circumference.

34. The circumference of a circle is supposed to be divided into 360 equal parts, called *degrees*, and marked °.

Each degree is divided into 60 equal parts, called *minutes*, and marked ′.

Each minute is divided into 60 equal parts, called *seconds*, and marked ″.

Thus, 31° 47′ 53″ means, 31 degrees, 47 minutes, 53 seconds;—that is, thirty-one 360ths of the circumference, forty-seven 60ths of one 360th; and fifty-three 60ths of the 60th of one 360th of the circumference.

35. The magnitude of any arc, in relation to the whole circumference, is at once indicated by stating the number of degrees, &c., which it contains. An arc of 39 degrees is $\frac{39}{360}$ of the circumference of which it is a part.

36. The equator and the parallels of latitude are circles ;* the meridian circles are nearly but not exact circles. The imaginary lines round the heavens, Equinoctial, Ecliptic, hour-circles, parallels of declination, are also circles. Hoops, rings, and the rims of vessels for holding liquids, are usually circles. The rims or edges of coins and of wheels are circles. When rotating (without moving out of its place) like water-wheels, every point in a wheel, also every point in the handle of a clock or watch, moves in a circle (that is, in the circumference of a circle) round its centre. The circle is considered one of the most perfect and beautiful of figures, has many curious properties, and is a figure of very great use in science and the arts.

Rectilineal Angles.

37. A PLANE RECTILINEAL ANGLE is the space between two straight lines lying in different directions and meeting at a point.

See below three such angles, each formed by two straight lines meeting at a point.

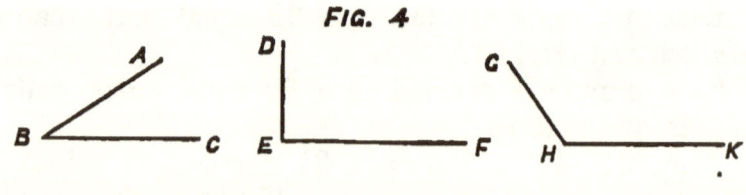

FIG. 4

---

* The word "circle" is often used to express the circumference alone, as well as the whole figure.

Such an angle is called *rectilineal*, because it is formed by straight lines, and *plane*, being all in one plane.

38. The angular point or *vertex* of an angle is the point of meeting of the lines which form the angle; these lines are called the *sides* of the angle.

An angle is named by a single letter at its vertex, or, when there is more than one angle at the same point, by a letter at the vertex between letters on each side.

The above angles may be called—

The angles	B,	E,	H,	or
"	ABC,	DEF,	GHK,	or
"	CBA,	FED,	KHG.	

39. There are other kinds of angles besides those formed of two straight lines and on a plane surface. For brevity, the word "angle" in this work will be taken to mean, "a plane rectilineal angle."

40. The magnitude of an angle shows the amount of difference in the directions of its sides. It is this difference which determines the angle, and not the length of the sides, which is immaterial.

41. Angles are quantities, and can be compared as to their magnitude, added, subtracted, &c.

FIG. 5

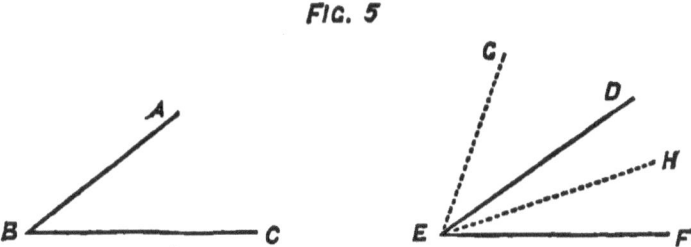

Suppose the angle B to be moved, the point B to be laid on the point E, and the line BC along the line EF : if, then, the line BA were to fall along the line ED, we should say that the angle B is exactly equal to the angle DEF.

If, the angles B and DEF being equal, we laid B on E, and BC along ED, the point A falling at the left of ED at G, the new angle formed, GEF, would be exactly double of ABC or DEF. In like manner, an angle might be trebled, and so on.

The line EH is manifestly much nearer to the direction of EF than ED is; accordingly, the angle DEF is considered greater than the angle HEF; GEF greater than DEF, and so on.

The angle GEH is obviously equal to the sum of the two angles GED, DEH. If we take the angle HEF from the angle DEF, the angle DEH is left; or the angle DEH is the difference between the angles DEF, HEF.

Angles can also be measured, and have their magnitudes defined with precision.

42. When the vertex of an angle is at the centre of a circle, the angle is said to *stand* on the arc included between its sides, and the arc is said to *subtend* or be *opposite to* the angle.—In fig. 3, p. 4, the angle ECA stands upon the arc EA; the angle ECB upon the arc EB; the arc DB subtends the angle DCB.

43. Let a thread be fixed at the centre C of the circle EABD, fig. 3, the circumference being supposed to be divided into degrees, which are numbered from D, so that we can know the length of any arc, reckoning from D. Let the thread be at first laid over the radius CD, and then carried round to B, A, and E, making an ever-increasing angle with CD. It will be found that *the arc between the thread and the point D increases just as the angle increases which the arc subtends.* This is an important truth in geometry.

When the angle is doubled, the arc on which it stands is doubled in length; when the angle is trebled, it stands on a arc of three times the number of degrees; and so on.

44. An arc of a circle is thus a correct measure of the angle at the centre which stands on it.

45. An angle is measured, therefore, by placing the vertex at the centre of a circle and measuring the number of degrees in the arc on which it stands. It is said to be an angle of that number of degrees. If, in fig. 3, the arcs AE, ED, DB, be arcs respectively of 65, 115, and 90 degrees, then ACE is an angle of 65°, ECD an angle of 115°, DCB an angle of 90°.

46. In the same or in equal circles, equal arcs are opposite to or subtend equal angles.

47. The magnitude of the circle makes no difference as to its use in the measurement of angles. An angle is the same whether its sides are long or short ; the arc on which it stands is of the same number of degrees, whether the circle be large or small. The degrees may be larger or less ; but the arc subtending the same angle is always the same part of the whole circumference ; that is, of the same number of degrees.

Varieties of Plane Rectilineal Angles.

48. A RIGHT ANGLE is an angle of 90°. The arc which subtends it is one-fourth of the circumference.

The angles ACB, BCD, in fig. 3, and E, fig. 4, are right angles.

49. A right angle is also the angle formed when one straight line stands upon another, so as to make the adjacent (side by side) angles equal — leaning neither towards one side nor the other.

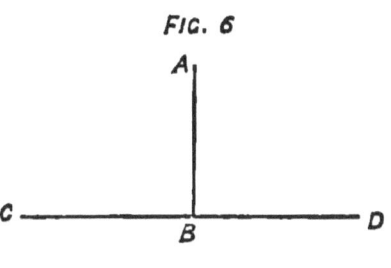

FIG. 6

AB makes the adjacent angles, ABC, ABD, equal

to each other; these then are right angles. If a circle were to be drawn with its centre at B, the angles at B would be found each to stand upon one-fourth of the circumference.

When there is only one angle, as E, fig. 4, p. 6, if it is a right angle, this will be best seen by producing (lengthening out) one of its sides, so as to make two adjacent angles that can be compared.

The corners of the leaves of books, of school-slates, of the wall, floor, or ceiling of a room, are (or ought to be) right angles.

50. A PERPENDICULAR to a straight line is a straight line making a right angle with it. Either side of a right angle is perpendicular to the other.

The perpendicular is the *distance;* that is, the shortest distance from a point to a line.

In the preceding figure, AB is perpendicular to CD; and is also the distance or shortest line from the point A to the line CD. Any other line drawn from A to CD is longer than AB.

51. AN ACUTE ANGLE is less than a right angle.

52. AN OBTUSE ANGLE is greater than a right angle.

In fig. 4, p. 6, the angle B is an acute angle, the angle H an obtuse angle.

FIG. 7

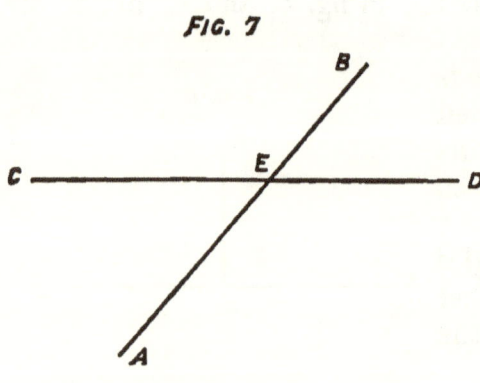

AEC = BED ; CEB = AED.

53. Angles such as AEC, BED, in the adjoining figure, are called *vertical* or *opposite* angles; also, AED, CEB.

54. Vertical or opposite angles are equal to one another.

55. CEB and CEA are *adjacent angles;* also, CEA and AED; AED and DEB; DEB and CEB.

56. When a straight line, as CE, makes two adjacent angles, CEA, CEB, with another line AB, each angle is called the *supplement* of the other, or supplementary to the other.

Two supplementary angles are together equal to two right angles. The supplement of an angle is the difference between it and two right angles.

Parallel Lines.

57. Parallel lines are lines everywhere at the same distance ; that is, if from any points in either, lines be drawn perpendicular to the other, these perpendiculars shall all be equal to each other.

FIG. 8

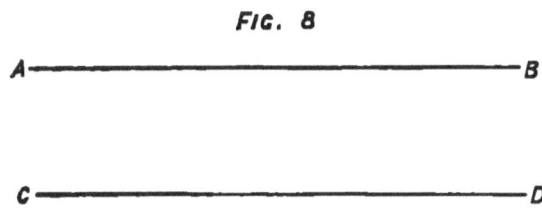

The straight lines, AB, CD, are parallel to each other, or, shortly, parallel.

Parallel lines continue at the same distance, however far they may be produced either way.

The top and bottom edges of the leaf of a book are parallel, or usually intended to be so.

PROBLEMS IN PRACTICAL GEOMETRY.

1. ELEMENTARY PROBLEMS.*

Problem 1.

58. *To draw a straight line on a plane between any two points in the plane.*

This is best done by help of the *flat ruler* or *straight edge.* The edge is placed as close as possible to both points, and a finely-pointed pencil is then drawn from point to point, touching both the edge and the surface on which the line is required.

It is well to test the straightness of the edge employed for drawing straight lines. This is done by first drawing with it a straight line extending its whole length; then, turn the ruler round, keeping the same side up, so that the ends of the edge with which the line was drawn exactly change places; and again draw a line with that edge. If the two lines coincide in every part, the edge may be considered straight.

The short expression, "Join AB," is generally used to signify, "Draw a straight line between the points A and B."

59. *Note.*—Any two points in a straight line are sufficient to determine its position.

Problem 2.

60. *To draw a circle, from any point as centre, with*

---

* It is recommended that the learner should insert every one of the following problems in an exercise book, giving the Enunciation of the problem, how to perform it, and the figure, constructed with neatness and accuracy. The figures should be large and cleanly drawn, as well as accurate. This book should be frequently examined by the teacher or guardian.

a radius equal to a given straight line, or to any given distance.

This is done by a *pair of compasses*, having a pencil or other marker firmly fixed to one of the legs. The legs are separated until the pencil point and other end are exactly at the required distance. The foot of one leg being then kept steadily on the point to be taken as centre, the pencil point is carried completely round the centre, gently touching the surface as it moves round, when it will mark on it the circumference of the required circle.

If carefully done, the pencil point will return exactly to the point from which it set out.

We are then said to *describe the circle from* the point taken as centre, and *with* a radius equal to the distance between the ends of the compasses.

Sometimes an *arc*, or part only of the circumference, is required. In this case, great care must be taken to keep the ends of the compasses at the same distance all the time.

61. *Note* 1.—It is manifest, from the construction, that all radii of the same circle are equal to one another ; also, that the radii of equal circles (33) are equal to each other.

62. *Note* 2.—It is manifest how, with this very useful instrument—a pair of compasses—we can perform the following operations :—

Find a point at a given distance from a given point.

Cut off from a line a part equal to any given line or distance.

Find two or more points at the same given distance from a given point, by drawing a circle, or arc of a circle, from the given point as centre.

63. *Note* 3.—The circumference of a circle gives a continuous series of points at any required distance from

a given point, and in every possible direction from it on the plane on which it is drawn. It is the *locus* or place of all the points on a plane equidistant from a given point in the plane.

Problem 3.

64. *To find a point at the same given distance (equidistant) from two given points.*

FIG. 9

Note.—The *given* distance must be not less than half the distance between the two given points.

Let A and B be the two given points, and the length of the line C the given distance.

It is required to find a point, D, whose distances from A and B shall each be equal to the line C.

From the centres A and B, with a radius equal to C, describe arcs cutting each other in D.

D is the point required. The distances, AD, BD, are each equal to the line C.

It is manifest that, on the other side of A and B, another point might be found the same distance from A and B as the length of the line C.

The problem would be impossible if the length of C were less than half the distance from A to B. The arcs would not meet.

Note.—It is plain that using radii differing in length, there may be found a great number of points in a plane, each equidistant from A and B.

Problem 4.

65. *To bisect a given angle; that is, to divide it into two equal angles.*

Let ABC be the angle to be bisected.

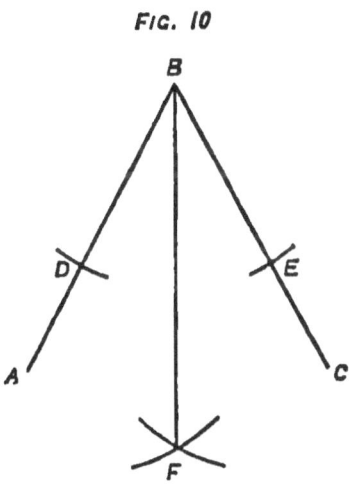

FIG. 10

In its sides AB, CB, take any two points equidistant from B, namely D and E (Note 2, Problem 2). By Problem 3, take the point F, equidistant from D and E. Join BF.

BF bisects the angle ABC, dividing it into two equal angles, ABF, CBF.

The problem may be quickly performed by using the same radius throughout.

Note 1.—The point F may be taken on the other side of D and E if necessary; even above B, without the angle; but it is best to take it as in the figure.

66. *Note* 2.—If DE be joined, it will be found to be bisected by BF, and to make right angles with it.

Problem 5.

67. *To bisect a straight line or an arc of a circle; that is, to divide it into two equal straight lines or two equal arcs.*

Let AB be the line (or arc) to be bisected.

Take a point C, equidistant from A and B, and, on the other side of AB, a point D, also equidistant from A and B. Join CD.

CD will cut AB in its middle point E, dividing it into two equal lines (or arcs), AE, BE.

The same radius may be used throughout.

If more convenient, C and D may be taken on the same side of AB, in which case CD must be produced till it meets AB; but it is best as in the figure.

Fig. II

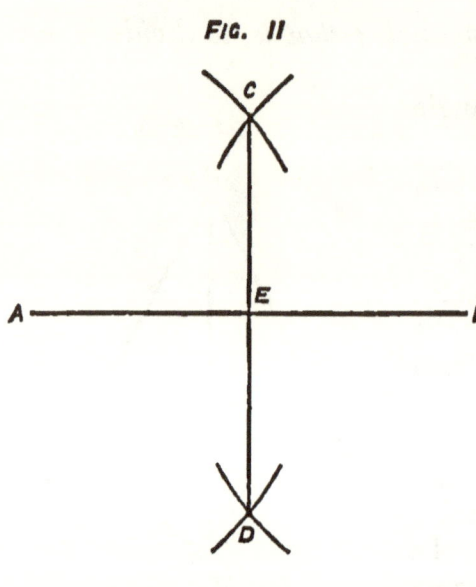

Note 1.—Observe that CD is at right angles to AB.

Note 2.—Observe that if CA and CB were joined, the problem is very similar to the last one, and the angle ACB would be bisected by CD.

68. *Second method.*—Another way of bisecting a line, much used, is by trial.

With one end of the compasses on one end of the line, put the other end of the compasses on the middle point of the line as nearly as can be guessed. Try if the parts thus taken are equal to each other. Perhaps one is less; then mark off on the greater, from the supposed middle point, a part equal to the less. By the eye, divide the small remainder into two equal parts; stretch out the compasses from the supposed middle of the line to the middle of the small part; try if this is a true half of the line, and so on.

Problem 6.

69. *To raise a perpendicular at a given point in a straight line.*

1. When the point is not far from the middle of the line.

Let AB be the line, and C the given point in it.

Take in AB points D and E, equidistant from C. By Problem 3, find a point F, equidistant from D and E. Join FC.

FC is the perpendicular required.

FIG. 12

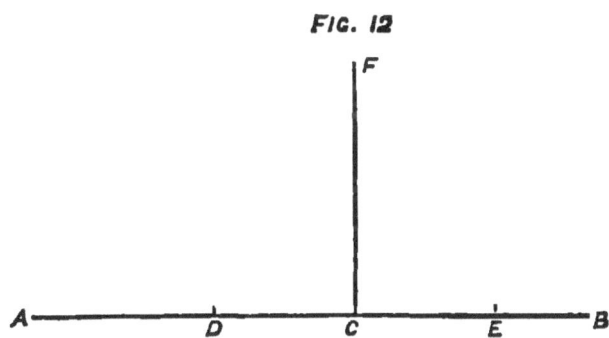

70. *Note.*—Not only F, but every point in the perpendicular FC, or in that line produced, is equidistant from D and E. In like manner, every point in CD, fig. 11, p. 16, is equidistant from A and B.

Every point in the perpendicular to a line (DE) *at its middle point is equidistant from the ends of the line;* or, that perpendicular is the *locus* of points equidistant from the ends of the line.

71. 2.—When the given point is at or near the end of the line :—

First method.—From any point, D (fig. 13), evidently some distance from where the perpendicular will fall, with DC as radius, describe the arc ECF, cutting AC in E and C. Draw ED, and produce it till it meets the arc in F (or till the produced part DF is equal to ED). Join FC.

FC is the perpendicular required.

72. *Note* 1.—This illustrates a curious and important property of the circle. EF is manifestly a diameter of

B

the circle drawn from the centre D with the radius
DC. *Now, any two straight lines, CE, CF, drawn*

FIG. 13

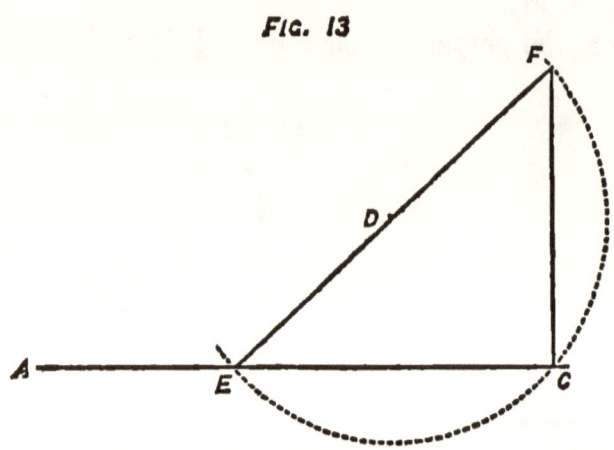

*from any point in the circumference to the ends of a
diameter, contain a right angle* (ECF) ; or, as usually
expressed, the angle in a semicircle (30) is a right angle.
73. *Second method.*—From C, with any radius, CD,

FIG. 14

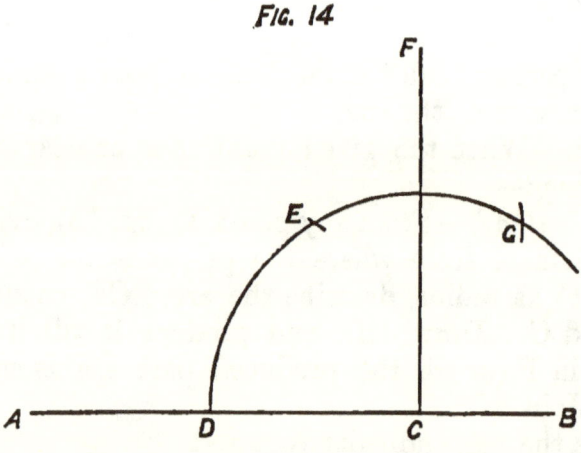

describe the arc DEG, cutting the line AB in D.
From D, with the same radius, cut the arc in E, and

from E, with the same radius, cut the arc again in G.
Find a point F, equidistant from E and G. Join
FC.

FC is the perpendicular required.

74. *Note* 2.—Builders, or others laying out ground,
sometimes employ the following method of making a
right angle :—Measure 3 yards by a cord from the given
point along the given line, fixing a peg at each end of
the three yards. Take two other cords, one of 4 yards,
the other of 5 yards ; fix one end of the 4-yard cord at
the peg where the right angle is required, and one end
of the 5-yard cord at the other peg. Then bring together the other ends of the 4 and 5-yard cords well
stretched. The 4-yard cord will be at right angles to
the 3-yard cord. This method may be applied on.paper
by the compasses, measuring 3 parts from a scale along
a line, and from its ends describing arcs crossing each
other, their radii being 4 and 5 parts.

75. *Note* 3.—*Any triangle* (figure of three straight
lines) *whose sides are in the proportion* 3, 4, 5 (as 6, 8,
10—9, 12, 15—15, 20, 25), *has the angle between the
two less sides a right angle.*

Problem 7.

76. *To draw a perpendicular to a straight line from
a point without it.*

Let AB be the line, and C the point without it.

1.—When the point without is nearly opposite to the
middle of the line.

From C, with any sufficient radius, describe an arc
cutting AB in D and E. Take a point, G, equidistant
from D and E. Join CG.

CG, cutting AB in F, is perpendicular to the line
AB.

77. *Note.*—The point F is the middle point of DE ;

and, as in the preceding cases, every point in CG is equidistant from D and E.

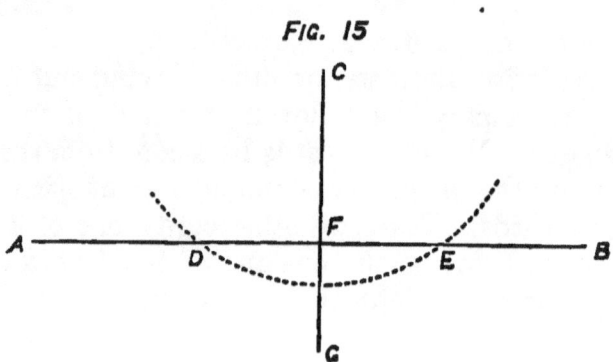

FIG. 15

78. 2.—When the point without is nearly opposite the end of the line.

First method.—From any point D, in AB, with the radius DC, describe an arc on the other side of AB;

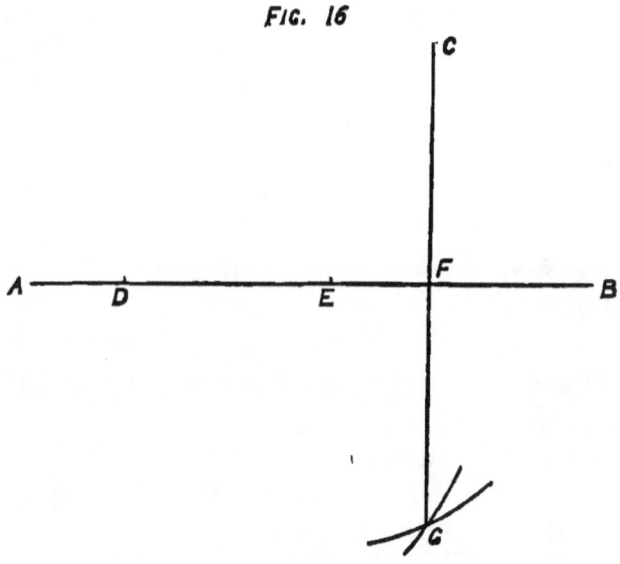

FIG. 16

from any other point, as E, in AB, with the radius EC, describe another arc cutting the former in G. Join CG.

CG, cutting AB in F, is the perpendicular required.

It will be better if the centres for the arcs, the points D and E, can be taken on different sides of the perpendicular, so far as can be judged as to its probable position.

79. *Second method.*—The point F, in AB, where the perpendicular falls, may be found in another way. From C, draw a straight line to D, a point in AB, some distance from where the perpendicular will fall. Bisect CD in H.* From H, with the radius HC or HD, describe an arc : it will cut AB in the point F.

80. *Note.*—The last method depends on the property of the circle referred to in Note 1, last Problem. CD is a diameter, and FD and FC are drawn to its ends from a point, F, in the circumference.

81. Right angles may also be drawn by the *square* or triangle, the limbs of which are set at right angles to each other ; and by the *flat ruler.* The latter has usually a line across it, at right angles to the edges. If this line be carefully laid *over* the line to which a perpendicular is wanted, the straight edge will be perpendicular to the line.

Problem 8.

82. *At a point in a straight line, to make an angle equal to a given angle.*

Let A be the point in the line AB, and C the given angle.

FIG. 17

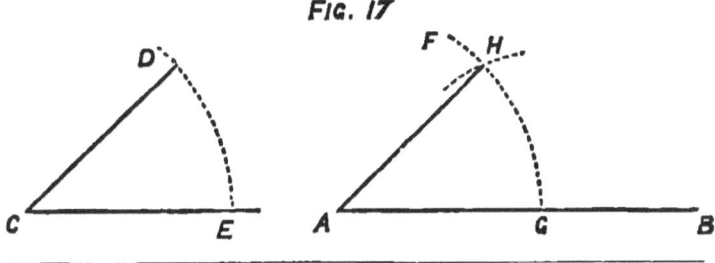

---

* The learner, looking at the last figure, can without difficulty *imagine* the line CD and its middle point H.

From A and C, with the same radius, describe the arcs FG, DE, cutting AB in G, and the sides of the angle C in D and E. From G, with a radius equal to the distance ED, cut the arc FG in H. Join AH.

The angle HAB will be equal to the angle C.

If BA were produced beyond A, an angle equal to C, having one side in BA produced, might be drawn at A, to lie the other way; also, two such angles might be drawn at A on the other side of AB.

83. *Note.*—The circles of which DE and FG are arcs are equal, being drawn with the same radius; and the arcs DE, HG were made equal, whence we have the angles C and A standing on these arcs also equal; illustrating Par. 46.

Problem 9.

84. *To trisect a right angle and a quadrantal arc* (the fourth part of the circumference); *that is, to divide each into three equal parts.*

Let ACB be the right angle (fig. 18). See Par. 48.

From C as centre, with any radius, CA, describe the arc AB. From A, with the same radius, cut the arc in the point 30°; and from B, with the same radius, cut the arc in the point 60°.

In the points 30° and 60°, the arc AB is divided into three equal parts of 30 degrees each.

Straight lines from these points in the arc to C will divide the right angle ACB into three equal angles, also of 30° each; for they stand upon three equal arcs of 30° each.

85. *Note.*—From B to 60°, along the arc, is two-thirds of 90°, or 60°; and a straight line from B to 60° on the arc would be the chord of 60°. The distance from B to 60° was made equal to CA, the radius; whence we see that *in a circle the chord of* 60° *is equal to the radius.*

Problem 10.

86. *To make a scale or line of chords.*

Draw CA at right angles to CB. From C, with any radius, as CA, draw the quadrantal arc AB.

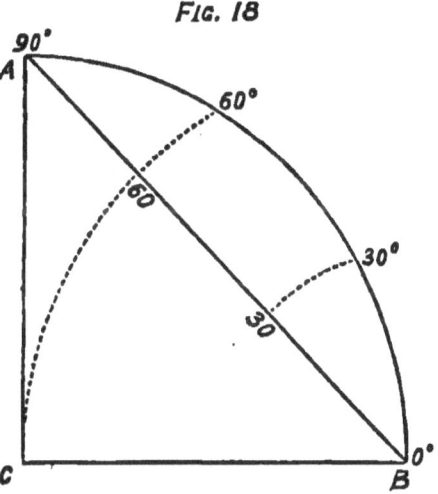

FIG. 18

Divide the arc AB into 90 equal parts. It is here divided into 3 equal parts, which is easily done by the preceding Problem. Further subdivision must be done by Prob. 5, and by trial.

Draw the chord AB. From the centre B, with successive radii to each division of the arc, describe arcs cutting the chord AB; and mark on the line AB the number of degrees taken as radius for each arc that cuts it.

The chord AB will then be a scale of chords, or line of chords, for a circle of which the radius is equal to CA, or to the chord of 60° on the scale.

Thus, in the illustrative figure above, with centre B and radius B 30°, describe the arc cutting AB in 30; with centre B and radius B 60°, describe an arc cutting AB in 60.

The straight line B 30, is manifestly equal to the chord of the arc B 30°; the line B 60 is equal to the chord of the arc B 60°; and were the straight line BA fully divided, each part of it, reckoning from B, would be the chord of the degrees marked at the end of the part.

The *scale of chords* is very useful for the construction

of angles of any required magnitude expressed in degrees. Such a scale is to be found on the flat rulers
sold by mathematical instrument makers.

Problem 11.

87. *At a point in a given line to make an angle of
any given number of degrees.*

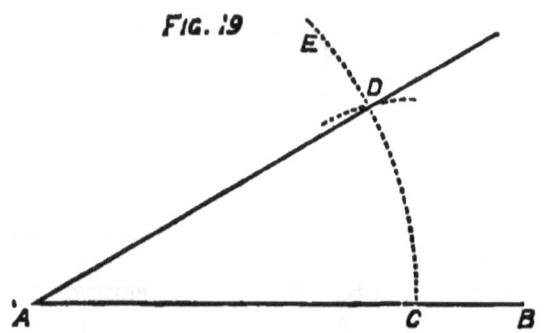

FIG. 19

Let A be the point in the line AB.

From the centre A, with a radius equal to the chord
of 60° from the line of chords, describe the arc EC,
cutting AB in C. From C as centre, with a radius
equal to the chord of the given number of degrees from
the same line of chords, describe an arc cutting the
former arc in D. Join AD.

The angle DAC will be an angle of the required
number of degrees.

The preceding is sufficient if the given angle is not
more than 90°.

If it is more than 90°, take it in two parts, each less
than 90°. Mark the chord of one, as from C to D ;
then mark the chord of the other part, from D towards
E, and draw a line from A to the point in the arc to
which the latter chord extends.

Problem 12.

88. *To measure the number of degrees in a given angle.*

Let ABC be the given angle.

From the centre C, with a radius equal to the chord of 60° on the line of chords, describe the arc AD. Lay the distance AD on the line of chords with the compasses ; the number it extends to will show the number of degrees in the arc AD and in the angle B.

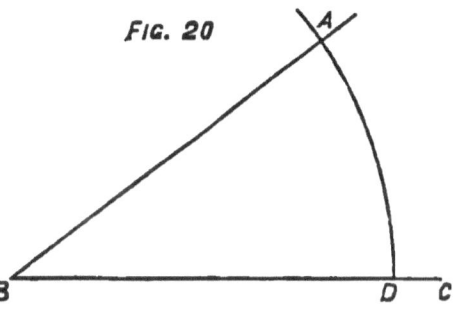

FIG. 20

If AD be greater than the line of chords, measure it in parts, and add.

Problem 13.

89. *At any distance from a straight line, to draw a straight line parallel to it.*

FIG. 21

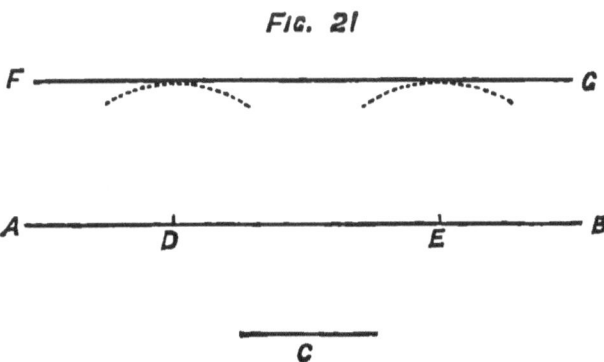

Let AB be the given straight line, and the length of the line C, the distance of the required parallel.

From D and E, any two points in AB, with the radius C, describe two arcs on the same side of AB.

Draw FG, just touching, but not cutting the arcs—a tangent (32) to both.

FG will be parallel to AB.

Problem 14.

90. *To draw through a given point a straight line parallel to a given straight line.*

FIG. 22

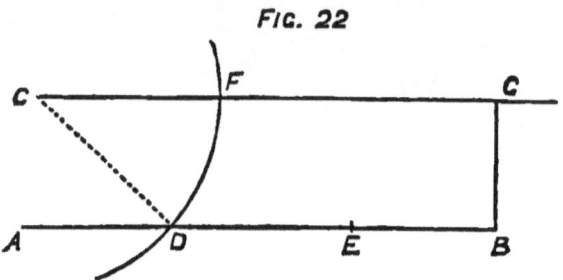

Let AB be the line, and C the point.

From C, with any radius of sufficient length, describe an arc cutting AB in D. With the same radius, from D, cut AB in E, and from E, cut the arc in F. Join CF.

CF will be parallel to AB.

Or, take any point D in AB; join CD; and at C, in the line CD, make the angle DCF equal to the angle CDA, by Problem 8.

CF will be parallel to AB.

91. *Note* 1.—This depends on the important geometrical truth that, *if a line* (CD) *meeting two others* (CF, AB) *makes the alternate angles equal* (ADC equal to DCF), *these two lines are parallel.*

Note 2.—Usually a line is drawn parallel to another by means of the instrument called "The Parallel Ruler." This may also be done by the "Square," or "Triangle," used to draw a right angle. If, from B, GB were drawn perpendicular to AB, a perpendicular to GB at G would be parallel to AB.

DEFINITIONS—SECOND SERIES.

Rectilineal, or Straight-lined Plane Figures.

92. There are three kinds of rectilineal plane figures —the triangle, the quadrilateral, and the polygon.

The Triangle.

93. A TRIANGLE is a plane figure contained by three straight lines, which are called its sides ; as, the triangle ABC.

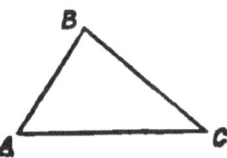

FIG. 23

94. There are seven things to be considered about a triangle—*the three sides, the three angles,* and *the area,* or extent of surface which it contains.

95. Any side is said to be *adjacent* to the angles which it aids in forming, and to *subtend* or be opposite to the other angle.

AB is adjacent to the angles A and B. It subtends, or is opposite to C.

96. One side of a triangle is sometimes called the *base;* the angular point opposite to the base is then called the *vertex* of the triangle : the angle there is called the *vertical angle.*

97. The ALTITUDE, or height of a triangle, is the perpendicular from one angular point on the opposite side,

FIG. 24

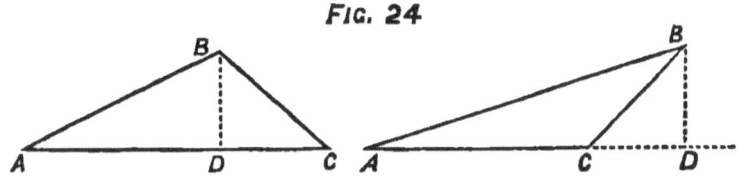

or on that side produced, which is then called "the base."

BD is the altitude in each of the triangles in fig. 24 ; in one, it falls without the triangle, the base AC being produced.

The distances from the perpendicular to the ends of the base are called *the segments* of the base ; that is, DA and DC in both figures.

Varieties of Triangles.

98. An acute angled triangle has all its angles acute.

99. An obtuse angled triangle has one obtuse angle. A triangle can only have one obtuse angle.

Fig. 23 is an acute angled triangle. Both triangles, ABC, in fig. 24, are obtuse angled.

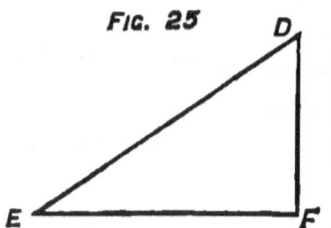

FIG. 25

100. A right angled triangle has one right angle. A triangle can only have one right angle. EDF is a right angled triangle.

101. In a right angled triangle, the side opposite the right angle is called *the hypotenuse.* The sides containing the right angle are often called *base* and *perpendicular.* ED is the hypotenuse.

102. An equilateral triangle has all its sides equal.

103. An isosceles triangle has two of its sides equal. The angle between the two equal sides is often called "the vertical angle," and the opposite side "the base."

The Quadrilateral.

104. A quadrilateral is a plane figure contained by four straight lines called its *sides.*

105. The diagonal of a quadrilateral is a straight line between two opposite angles. Every quadrilateral

may have two diagonals ; as, in fig. 26, a straight line
from A to C, or from B to D.

106. There are three kinds of quadrilaterals—the
parallelogram, the trapezoid, and the trapezium.

The Parallelogram.

107. A parallelogram is a quadrilateral of which the
opposite sides are parallel.

The figure ABCD
(called also AC, or
BD), and the next three
figures are parallelo-
grams.

Fic. 26

108. The opposite
sides of every parallelogram are equal ; the opposite
angles also are equal ; and a diagonal divides it into
two triangles equal in all respects.

BC is equal to AD ; AB to CD. The angles A and
C are equal, also the angles B and D. A diagonal, as
BD, divides ABCD into two triangles, ABD, CBD,
equal in all respects.

109. There are four kinds of parallelograms—the
square, the rectangle, the rhombus, the rhomboid.

110. A SQUARE is a parallelogram
having all its sides equal, and all its
angles right angles. EFGH is a square.

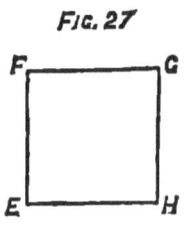

Fic. 27

A square is spoken of as the square
of any of its sides. The adjoining
figure may be called the square of EH,
or the square of EF, &c. And it may
be expressed shortly EH², or EF².

The square is a figure of great use in geometry. In
mensuration it is taken as the unit of measure for
expressing the areas of figures.

111. A RECTANGLE (or oblong) is a parallelogram

having its angles right angles, but its adjacent sides
unequal. KLMN is a rectangle.

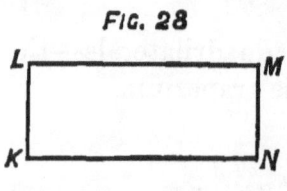

FIG. 28

A rectangle is said to be contained by any two of its adjacent
sides. The rectangle KLMN, is
contained by the lines KL, LM,
or LM, MN. It may be expressed
shortly, the rectangle KL.LM,
KL.KN, or LM.MN; or, the rectangle under KL and KN.

School slates, the boards and leaves of books, the walls
of rooms and panes of windows, are usually rectangles.

112. A RHOMBUS is a parallelogram having all its

FIG. 29

sides equal, but its angles not
right angles.

OPQR is a rhombus.

113. A RHOMBOID is a parallelogram having its adjacent sides
unequal and its angles not right
angles. The figure ABCD (26)
is a rhomboid.

114. Any side of a parallelogram may be taken as
base. Often it is the lower of the sides parallel to the
bottom of the page.

115. THE ALTITUDE of a parallelogram is the perpendicular on the base, or on the base produced, from
any point in the opposite side. It expresses the distance between these sides.

116. In rectangles, if any side be taken as base, the
adjacent side is the altitude, being a perpendicular from
the opposite side. In squares, the length of the side
expresses both base and altitude.

The Trapezoid.

117. A TRAPEZOID is a quadrilateral, of which only
two sides are parallel.

118. The *altitude* of a trapezoid is the distance between the parallel sides; that is, the perpendicular between them.

STUV is a trapezoid, the sides, TU, SV, being parallel, the other two not parallel. TX is the altitude, which may be drawn from any point in TU to SV, or, if necessary, to SV produced.

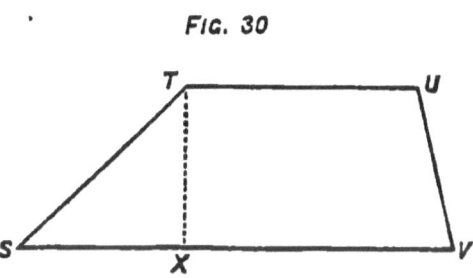

FIG. 30

The Trapezium.

119. A TRAPEZIUM is a quadrilateral of which no two sides are parallel; often termed, simply, "A quadrilateral."

Note.—Polygons are referred to afterwards.

2. PROBLEMS FOR THE CONSTRUCTION OF TRIANGLES AND QUADRILATERALS.

Problem 15.

120. *To construct a triangle, the sides of which shall be equal, each to each,* to three given straight lines, of which any two must be together greater than the third.*

For there cannot be a triangle in which any two sides are not greater than the third.

Let A, B, C be the three given straight lines.

---

* In this (and similar cases), the expression, "each to each," is used to denote that one given line shall be equal to one side of the triangle, another given line to another side, and so on ;—not merely that the sum of the three lines shall be equal to the sum of the three sides, which might be, and yet not one line equal to any side of the triangle.

Draw a straight line DE, equal to any one of them, as C.

From D as centre, with a radius equal to A, describe an arc; and from E as centre, with a radius equal to

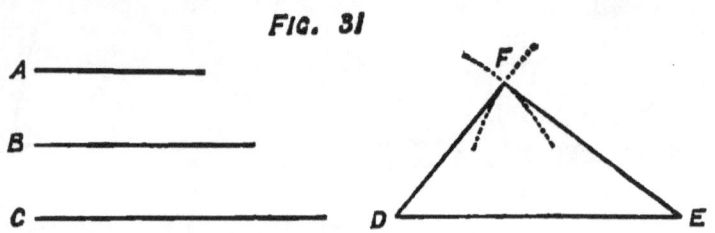

FIG. 31

B, describe an arc cutting the other arc in F.   Join FD, FE.

DEF is the triangle required.   DE is equal to C, DF equal to A, FE equal to B.

In like manner, an isosceles or equilateral triangle may be drawn.

The triangle might have been drawn to lie the other way, by making DF equal to B, and EF equal to A; also, two like triangles might be constructed on the other side of DE; and A or B might have been taken as base, instead of C.

121. *Corollary.** From the preceding Problem, it is obvious how—

To find a point (F) at any given distances (A and B) from two given points (D and E), provided that the sum of the given distances is greater than the distance between the two given points.

122. *Note.—To make a triangle equal in all respects to any given triangle.*

Make a triangle having its sides equal, each to each, to the sides of the given triangle; for it is a geometrical truth, that—

---

* Something that is manifest, or follows easily from what has gone before.

When two triangles have all their sides equal, each to each, they are equal in all respects ; that is—
1. Their sides are equal, each to each.
2. The angles opposite to equal sides are equal.
3. Their areas are equal.

Problem 16.

123. *To construct a triangle, any two sides and the contained angle being given.*

The construction is obvious. Make an angle equal to the given angle, having its sides equal, each to each, to the given sides, and join the ends of the sides.

124. *Note.*—Hence another method of making a triangle equal in all respects to a given triangle—

Make two sides and the contained angle equal, each to each, to like parts in the given triangle, and join the ends of the sides ; for—

Two triangles are equal in all respects when they have two sides and the included angle in one equal, each to each, to like parts in the other.

Problem 17.

125. *To construct any quadrilateral, the four sides being given, and one angle, included in two specified sides.*

As in the preceding problem, make an angle equal to the given angle, with sides of the given length. Then, by cor. Problem 15, find a point at distances from the ends of these sides, equal to the other two given sides, placing the required sides adjacent, and join this point and the ends of the sides containing the given angle.

126. Thus may be formed a trapezium, a rhombus, a rhomboid, a square, a rectangle.

In the four last, if two adjacent sides are known, all four sides are known, as in every parallelogram the opposite sides are equal.

C

Example.—To form a rectangle, the sides being equal to the lines A and B.

FIG. 32

Draw the right angle DCF, having CD equal to A, CF equal to B.

From D, with a radius equal to CF or B, describe an arc ; and from F, with a radius equal to CD or A, describe an arc cutting the former in E.   Join DE, EF.—CDEF is the rectangle required.

In like manner, a rhomboid is made.

In constructing a rhombus or square, the sides are all equal, and the same radius is used for both arcs.

Problem 18.

127. *To construct a square, the diagonal being given.*

Bisect the diagonal.   Through its middle point draw a perpendicular both ways, making the part on each side equal to the half diagonal.   The lines joining the ends of the diagonal to the ends of the perpendicular will form the square required.

The perpendicular will be the other diagonal.

Note.—From this it will be seen that *the diagonals of a square are equal, and intersect each other at right angles.*

Problem 19.

128. *To construct a triangle when one side and the adjacent angles are given ; the sum of the two angles being less than two right angles.*

At one end of the given line make an angle equal to one of the given angles.   At the other end, on the same side of the line, make an angle equal to the other given angle.   The sides of these angles, when produced, will meet and form the required triangle.

129. *Note* 1.—Hence another method of making a triangle equal in all respects to a given triangle—

Make any side and the adjacent angles equal, each to each, to like parts in the given triangle; for—

Two triangles are equal in all respects when they have a side and the adjacent angles in one equal, each to each, to like parts in the other.

130. *Note* 2.—It is an important truth in geometry that—

The interior angles of every triangle are together equal to two right angles;—

Whence, any two of them must be less than two right angles.

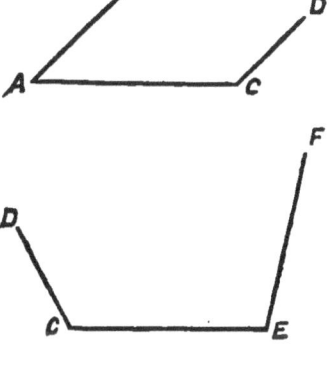

If the two adjacent angles at the ends of a line were exactly equal to two right angles, their sides would be parallel, and would not meet, however far produced either way; as, AB, CD.

If they were together greater than two right angles, their sides would diverge when produced; as, CD, EF.

Problem 20.

131. *To construct a right-angled triangle.*

1. When the base and perpendicular are given; as, AC and CB (fig. 33).

This is a case of Problem 16.

132. 2. When the base (or perpendicular) and an acute angle are given.

(1.) When the given side is between the two given angles (right and acute); as, AC, and the angles BAC, and C being given.

This is a case of Problem 19.

(2.) When the given side is opposite to the given acute angle; as, AC and the angle required at B.

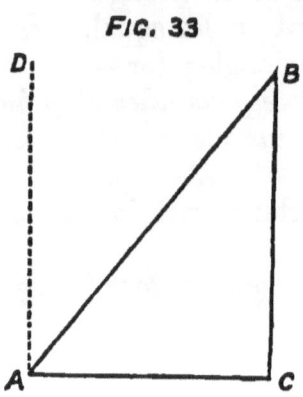

FIG. 33

At A and C draw AD and CB perpendicular to AC. At A in the line AD, make the angle DAB equal to thé given acute angle, producing AB till it meets the perpendicular at C in B.

The angle at B will be equal to the given acute angle.

If the acute angle required at B is given in degrees, subtract it from 90°; the difference will give the angle BAC; we may then proceed by Problems 11 and 19.

133. 3. When the hypotenuse and a side are given; as, AB and AC.

At one end of the given side, as C, raise a perpendicular. From the other end A, as centre, with a radius equal to the hypotenuse, draw an arc, cutting the perpendicular in B. Join AB.

134. 4. When the hypotenuse and an acuté angle are given; as, AB and B.

At one end of the hypotenuse, as B, make an angle equal to the given angle; from the other end, A, let fall a perpendicular, AC, on the other side of the acute angle.

Or, having made the acute angle (at B), bisect the hypotenuse; from its middle point, with its half as radius, describe a semicircle; join the point (C) where the arc cuts the side of the acute angle to the other end (A) of the hypotenuse (72).

135. *Note* 1.—In a right-angled triangle, there is always one angle known—the right angle. As all the angles of the triangle are together equal to two right

angles, the two acute angles must be together equal to one right angle ; and one of them is equal to the difference between the other and one right angle.

Note 2.—In every right-angled triangle, the half of the hypotenuse is equal to the line from its middle point to the right angle.

Problem 21.

136. *To describe a rectangle, the diagonal and a side being given.*

By case 3 of the preceding problem, make a right-angled triangle, having the hypotenuse equal to the diagonal, and a side equal to the given side. Then, by Problem 15, make an equal triangle on the other side of the hypotenuse, taking care that, in the figure formed, the equal sides are opposite, not adjacent.

The quadrilateral composed of the two triangles will be the required rectangle.

Or, having made the right-angled triangle as above, through the ends of the hypotenuse, draw lines parallel to the sides of the triangle.

137. *Note.*—The diagonal divides every parallelogram into two triangles equal in all respects, so that if one of these is known, the whole is easily formed.

Problem 22.

138. *To make a rectangle, rhombus, rhomboid, or any quadrilateral, when the diagonal and sides are known.*

It is manifest from the preceding note, that, in the case of the rhombus, rhomboid, or rectangle, this is simply making on opposite sides of the same line (the diagonal) two triangles with equal given sides, as in Problem 15. In the case of the rectangle and rhomboid, care must be taken that the equal sides are opposite, not adjacent. In the case of the trapezium, the triangles are different ; but still use Problem 15.

Problem 23.

139. *To construct a triangle, given the base, the per-pendicular on the base from the opposite angle, and the place where the perpendicular meets the base.*

The construction is obvious. Having drawn the base and the perpendicular of the given length and at the given point in the base, join the end of the perpendicular to the ends of the base.

Problem 24.

140. *To form a trapezium, the diagonal being given; also the perpendiculars on it from the opposite angles, and the places of these on the diagonal.*

The construction is obvious from the preceding problem.

3. PROBLEMS FOR THE CONSTRUCTION OF RECTILINEAL FIGURES EQUAL IN AREA TO OTHERS, THOUGH UN-EQUAL IN OTHER RESPECTS.

(Sometimes called *equivalent* figures.)

Problem 25.

141. *To make a rectangle equal to a given parallelogram.*

Let ABCD be the given parallelogram.

Through A and D draw AE and DF at right angles to AD, and meeting the opposite side, or that side produced, in E and F.

AEFD will be a rectangle, and it will be equal in area to ABCD.

Another rectangle, equal to ABCD, might be constructed by drawing perpendiculars to AB at A and B to meet CD or that line produced.

142. *Note.*—This illustrates the important geometrical truth, that—

Parallelograms on the same base and between the same parallels are equal to one another; that is, equal in area.

FIG. 34

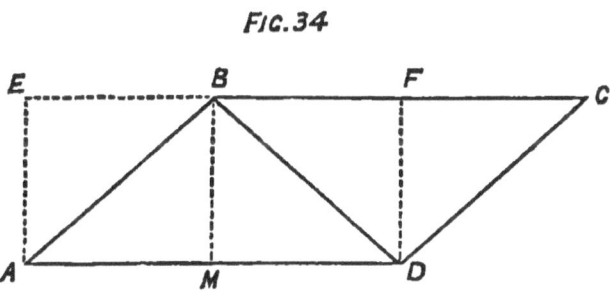

AEFD and ABCD are on the same base AD and between the same parallels AD and EC. The parts of the whole figure that do not form part of both, are manifestly equal—the triangles AEB, DFC.

Or,—parallelograms are equal whose bases and altitudes are equal.

Problem 26.

143. *To make a rectangle equal to a given triangle.*

Let ABD in the preceding figure be the given triangle.

Bisect AD in M. Through M and D draw MB and DF at right angles to AD. Through B draw BC parallel to AD.

MBFD will be a rectangle, and it will be equal to the triangle ABD.

144. *Note.*—*A triangle is half of any parallelogram on the same base and between the same parallels* (or, of the same base and altitude).

Whence, the triangle ABD is half of the rectangle AEFD, and must be equal to the rectangle MBFD, which is obviously the half of the rectangle AEFD.

145. It is manifest that the two rectangles AEBM and MBFD are equal; and their bases are equal, as AD was bisected in M.

This illustrates the geometrical truth, that *parallelograms on equal bases and between the same parallels are equal.*

Problem 27.

146. *To make a parallelogram equal to a given triangle, and having an angle equal to a given angle.*

Let ABC be the given triangle, and D the given angle.

Fic. 35

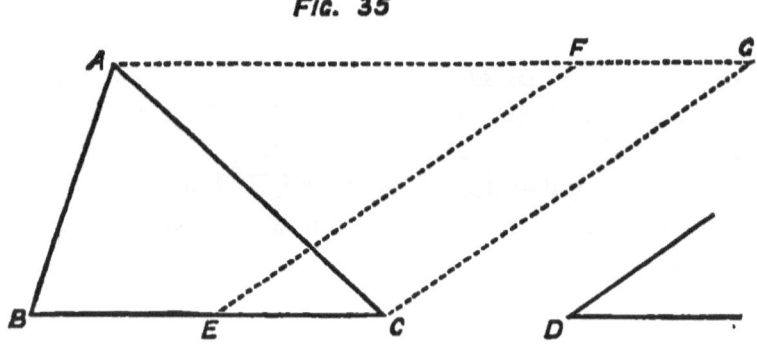

Bisect BC in E. At E in the line EC, make the angle FEC, equal to the angle D. Through C draw CG parallel to EF, and through A draw AG parallel to BC.

EFGC is a parallelogram; it is equal to the triangle ABC, and its angles FEC and G are equal to the angle D.

Problem 28.

147. *To make a triangle equal in area to a given quadrilateral.*

Let ABCD be the given quadrilateral.

Draw CA, joining the ends of any two adjoining

sides, BC, BA.   Through B draw BE, parallel to CA, meeting DA produced in E.   Join EC.

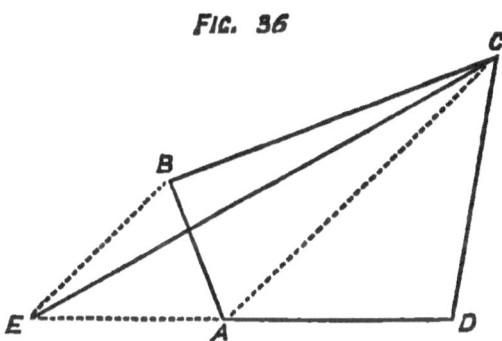

FIC. 36

The triangle ECD is equal to the quadrilateral ABCD.

Note.—This depends on the geometrical truth, that—

Two triangles (ABC, AEC), *on the same base* (AC) *and between the same parallels* (AC, EB), *are equal.*

These two triangles being equal, add the triangle ACD to each ; then, the whole triangle ECD is equal to the figure ABCD.

148. *Cor.* 1.—To reduce a given rectilineal figure to another, equal in area, but with one side less.

This is done in the present problem.   The same construction will apply, however many sides there may be from C by D to A.   Let any two adjacent sides be treated as AB and BC in this problem.

149. *Cor.* 2.—To reduce any polygon to an equal triangle.

By the preceding corollary reduce it to an equal polygon with one side less ; do the same with the polygon thus obtained, and so on.

Problem 29.

150. *On a given straight line to make a triangle equal in area to a given triangle.*

Let ABC be the given triangle and F the given line.

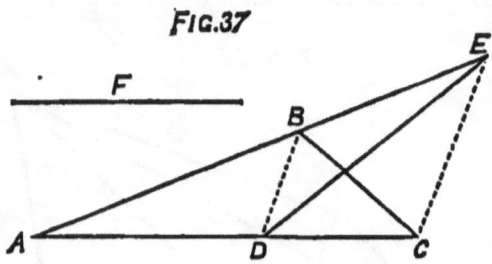

FIG.37

Take in AC, AD, equal to F. Join BD. Through C draw CE parallel to BD, meeting AB produced in E. Join DE.

The triangle AED is equal in area to the triangle ABC. If necessary, on F, which is equal to AD, make a triangle with its sides equal to those of the triangle AED, as in Problem 15. It will be equal in area to AED, and therefore to ABC.

Note.—If F is greater than AC, take AD equal to F in AC produced, and proceed as before.

Problem 30.

151. *From a point in a side of a given triangle, to draw a straight line which shall divide the triangle into two equal parts.*

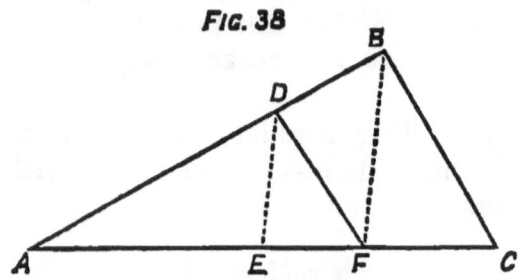

FIG. 38

Let ABC be the given triangle, and D, in AB, the given point.

Bisect AC in E, and join DE. Through B draw BF parallel to DE, meeting AC in F. Join DF.

The line DF divides the triangle ABC into two equal parts, ADF and BDFC.

152. *Note.*—If the given point is at one of the angular points, join it to the middle point of the opposite side. If it is at the middle of a side, join it to the opposite angular point; for—

The straight line from the vertex of any angle of a triangle to the middle of the opposite side divides the triangle into two equal parts.

Problem 31.

153. *To find the side of a square equal to the sum of two given squares.*

Draw a right angle having its sides equal, each to each, to the sides of the given squares. Join the ends of the sides, forming the hypotenuse of a right-angled triangle.

The square of the hypotenuse thus found will be equal to the sum of the two given squares.

154. *Note.*—This illustrates an important proposition, referred to more particularly under "Mensuration," namely—

The square of the hypotenuse of any right-angled triangle is equal to the sum of the squares of the two other sides.

Problem 32.

155. *To find the side of a square equal to the sum of several given squares.*

Let AB, BC, BE, be the sides of squares. It is required to find a single line, DE, the square of which shall be equal to the sum of the squares of AB, BC, and BE.

By the preceding problem, find AC the side of a

square equal to the squares of two of the given lines, AB, BC—B being a right angle.

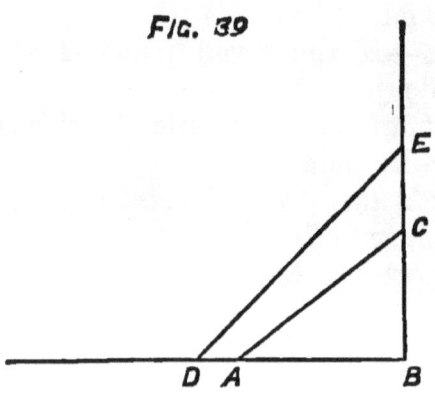

FIG. 39

Then, in one side of the right angle take BD equal to AC, and in the other side, BE equal to another of the given lines. Join DE.

A square, of which the side is equal to DE, will be equal to the sum of the three squares of which the sides are respectively equal to AB, BC, and BE.

Proceed in like manner ; setting off the length of DE on BD produced, and the length of the side of a fourth square on BE, or that side produced, if necessary.

Problem 33.

156. *To find the side of a square equal to the differ-ence of two given squares.*

Let AC, preceding figure, be a side of the greater of the given squares. Bisect it, and on it describe a semi-circle. From the end A, with a radius equal to the side of the other given square, cut the semicircle, sup-pose in B. Join BC.

BC will be the side of a square equal to the differ-ence between the squares of AC and AB.

Problem 34.

157. *To find the side of a square equal to half of a given square.*

Draw the diagonals of the given square : they bisect each other at right angles.

The square of the half diagonal will be equal to half of the given square.

Or, bisect the side of the given square, and at the point of bisection raise a perpendicular equal to the half side. The line joining the end of the perpendicular to either end of the side, will be the side of a square equal to half of the given square.

Problem 35.

158. *To make a square equal to a rectangle of which the sides are given.*

Let AB, BC, the sides of the given rectangle, be placed in one straight line AC. Bisect AC in the point D, and from the centre D, with the radius AD, on AC describe a semicircle. At B draw BE at right angles to AC, meeting the arc in E.

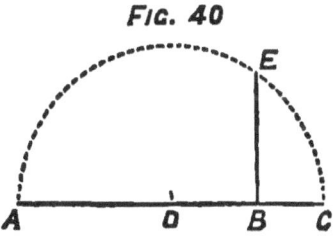

FIG. 40

The square of BE is equal to the rectangle contained by the lines AB, BC.

Note.—If the lengths of the sides are given in numbers, multiply the sides, and extract the square root of the product. This will give the length of the side of a square equal to a rectangle under the given sides.

Thus, let the sides of a rectangle be respectively 4 and 25. The product of 4 and 25 is 100 ; the square root of 100 is 10. Then a square of which the side is 10 is exactly equal to a rectangle, of which the sides are 4 and 25 ; or equal to any rectangle, the product of whose sides is 100 ; as, sides 8 and 12½ ; 5 and 20 ; 16 and 6¼ ; and so on.

4. PROBLEMS RELATING TO THE CIRCLE.

Problem 36.

159. *To find the centre of a given circle.*
Draw any chord ; bisect it. Through the point of bisection, draw a chord at right angles to it. The second chord will be a diameter, and its middle point will be the centre of the circle.

160. *Note.*—A straight line drawn from the centre of a circle to the middle point of any chord, is at right angles to it. If a straight line be drawn from the centre at right angles to a chord, it will also bisect the chord.

Problem 37.

161. *To describe a circle through any three given points, not in the same straight line.*
Let A, B, D be the three given points. Join any one to the other two, as B to A and D, forming

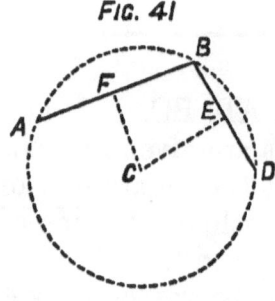

FIG. 41

the straight lines BA, BD. Bisect these lines in E and F. Draw perpendiculars to them at the points of bisection, E and F, meeting in the point C. C will be equidistant from the three, A, B, and D ; and a circle drawn from C as centre, with CA, CB, or CD as radius, will pass through all three points.

162. *Note* 1.—This problem shows how to find a point equidistant from three given points not in the same straight line.

163. *Note* 2.—It shows also how to describe a circle about a given triangle ; that is, passing through its angular points. Bisect any two sides, and so on as above.

Problem 38.

164. *To find the centre of a circle, only an arc of it being given.*

Take any three points in the arc, and proceed with these as in Problem 37. The point in which the perpendiculars meet will be the centre of the circle.

Problem 39.

165. *To draw a tangent to a circle at a given point in the circumference.*

Let B be the given point.

Find the centre of the circle, C. Join CB. A perpendicular to CB at B will be a tangent to the circle at B ; that is, will touch the circle at the point B, every other point in the line being without the circle.

166. *Note.*—Any straight line from the centre of a circle to the point of contact of a tangent is at right angles to the tangent ; and any straight line at right angles to a tangent at its point of contact passes through the centre.

Problem 40.

167. *To draw a tangent to a circle from a given point without it.*

Let B be the point without the circle (fig. 42).

Find the centre, C. Join BC, and bisect that line in D. From the centre D, on BC describe a semicircle, cutting the circle in E. Join BE.

The straight line BE is a tangent to the circle, and it is drawn from the point B.

Note 1.—From the same point, another tangent may

evidently be drawn, to the point where a semicircle on
the other side of BC would cut the circle. These two
tangents would be equal.

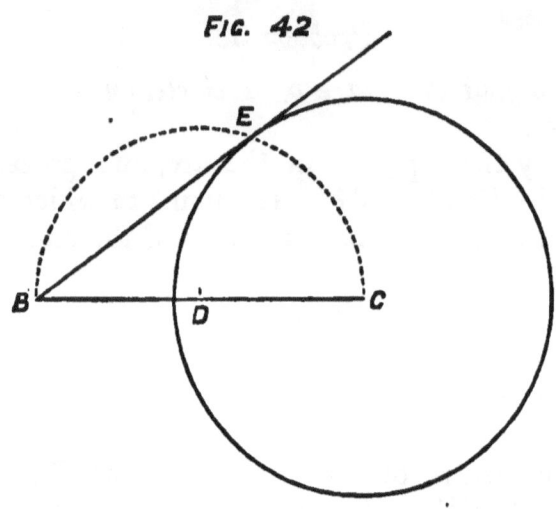

FIG. 42

168. *Note* 2.—If EC were drawn, the angle BEC
would be a right angle, being the angle in the semicircle BEC (72);—a line from the centre of a circle is
always perpendicular to a tangent at the point of
contact.

Problem 41.

169. *On a given straight line to describe a segment of
a circle containing an angle equal to a given angle.*

Let AB be the given straight line, and H the given
angle.

At B make the angle ABD equal to H.   Bisect AB
in E.   At E and B draw perpendiculars to AB and BD
meeting in C.   From C, with the radius CB, describe
the circle BFAG.

The segment AFB will contain an angle equal to H ;
that is, lines from any point in the arc BFA to A and
B, as FA, FB, will contain an angle equal to H.

170. *Note.*—This illustrates two remarkable proper-ties of the circle.

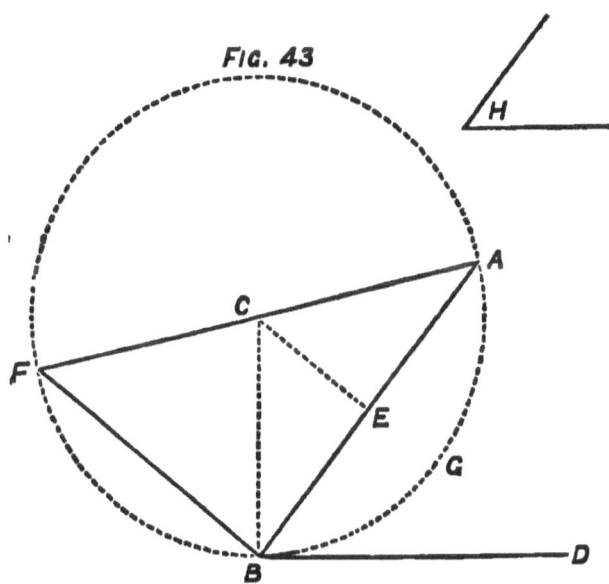

FIG. 43

1. *The angle* (ABD) *made by a chord* (AB) *and a tangent* (BD) *is equal to any angle* (F) *in the alternate segment of the circle* (BFA).

2. *Angles in the same segment of a circle are equal to another;* that is, the angles formed by lines to A and B, from any points in the arc of the segment BFA, are equal.

5. Problems relating to the Proportions of Lines and Figures.

DEFINITIONS—THIRD SERIES.

(First, read Article 274, &c., on Proportion, in the Algebra.)

171. Similar figures are those which have the same shape or form, though they may differ in magnitude.

D

A man and a boy are similar figures ; a house and a well-constructed model of it are similar figures ; or, a machine and a model of it.

Any two squares are similar ; any two equilateral triangles are similar ; any two circles are similar.

172. Similar rectilineal figures have the angles of one equal, each to each, to the angles of the other, and the corresponding sides, about the equal angles, in the same proportion ; that is, any two sides in one triangle are in the same proportion as the *corresponding sides* (173) in the other triangle.

FIG. 44

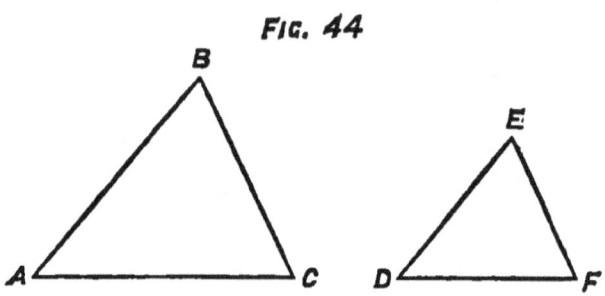

The triangles ABC, DEF, are similar. Their angles are equal, each to each—namely, A = D ; B = E ; C = F ; and the sides about the equal angles are in the same proportion ; those opposite equal angles being the *antecedents,* or *consequents* of the ratios—

AB : AC :: DE : DF.

173. AB and AC are *corresponding sides* to DE and DF. They are the sides of equal angles, A and D. AB corresponds to DE, being opposite equal angles, C and F. AC and DF correspond ; they are opposite the equal angles B and E. To say that sides correspond, means that they are similarly situated in respect to equal angles. AB and DE, opposite the equal angles C and F, are the *antecedents* of the ratios ;

AC and DF, opposite the equal angles B and E, are the *consequents* of the ratios.

Problem 42.

174. *To divide a straight line into any number of equal parts.*

Let AB be the line, to be divided into five equal parts.

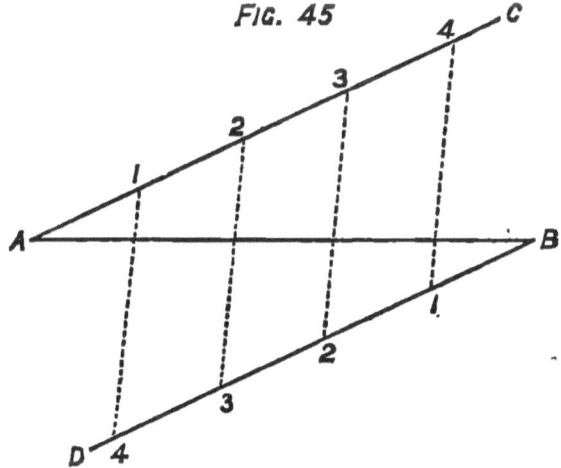

FIG. 45

Through A and B, draw AC and BD parallel to each other, on opposite sides of AB.

From A towards C, lay off on AC four equal parts— one less than the number given—A 1, 1—2, 2—3, 3—4; and the same number of the same length each, from B towards D, on BD.

Join 4, the last point marked on AC, to 1, the first marked on BD, 3 to 2, 2 to 3, and 1 to 4. These cross lines will divide the line AB into five equal parts.

175. *Note.*—This may be done in a simpler manner, but requiring a greater number of lines to be drawn parallel to each other.

Lay off five equal parts on any line, AF, making an

angle with AB,—namely, A 1, 1—2, 2—3, 3—4, 4—F.
Join BF. Through the four points of division, draw
lines parallel to BF. These will divide AB into five
equal parts.

176. *Note.*—This illustrates the geometrical truth,
that—

*Parallel lines cut diverging lines in the same pro-
portion.*

The points, 1, 2, 3, 4, divide the line AF into five
equal parts, and the parallel lines drawn through these
points divide the line AB in the same proportion; that
is, into five equal parts.

Problem 43.

177. *To divide a straight line into any number of
equal parts, without drawing parallel lines.*

Let it be desired to divide AB into five (or n) equal
parts.

Draw any line AC, making an acute angle with AB.

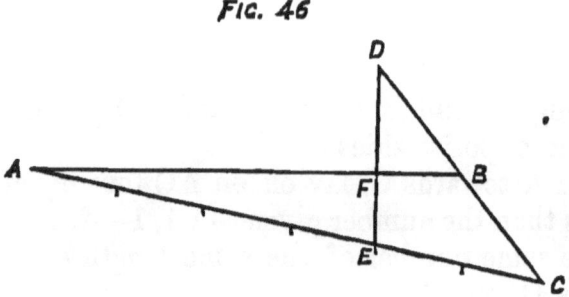

FIG. 46

On it lay off six ($n + 1$) equal parts. Let E be the end
of the 4th ($n - 1$th) part, reckoning from A. Join CB,
and produce it till the produced part (BD) is equal to
CB. Join DE.

From B to the point F, where DE cuts AB, will be
one-fifth of AB.

Problem 44.

178. *To find a fourth proportional to three given straight lines.*

Let AB, BC, and AD be the lines; it is required to find a fourth line, x, such that—

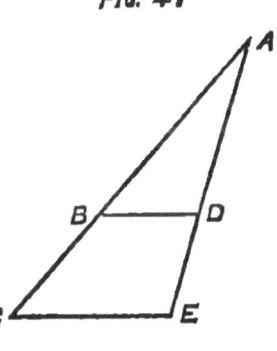

FIG. 47

AB : BC :: AD : x.

Place AB and BC in the same straight line, and AD making an angle with AC. Join BD, and through C, draw CE parallel to BD, meeting AD produced in E. DE is the line required; that is—

AB : BC :: AD : DE.

Note.—This illustrates the above geometrical truth (176). BD parallel to CE, cuts AC and AE in the same proportion. •

Problem 45.

179. *To find a third proportional to two given straight lines*, AB, BC, last figure ; that is, a line, x, such that—

AB : BC :: BC : x.

Place AB and BC in one straight line. Draw AD equal to BC, and making any angle with AC. Join BD. Through C draw CE parallel to BD. DE is the line required; that is, AB : BC :: BC (or AD) : DE.

Problem 46.

180. *To find a mean proportional between two given straight lines*, AB and BC, fig. 40, page 45 ; that is, to find a straight line, x, such that—

AB : x :: x : BC.

This is done in Problem 35, page 45. Proceed exactly as is done in that problem. BE is the line required.

AB : BE :: BE : BC.

Note.—If EA, EC, fig. 40, were joined, AEC would be a triangle, right-angled at E (72). Whence it appears that if from the right angle of a right-angled triangle a perpendicular be drawn to the hypotenuse, the perpendicular is a mean proportional between the segments of the hypotenuse. Farther, such perpendicular divides the triangle into two triangles similar to the large triangle and to each other.

Problem 47.

181. *To divide a straight line, so that one part is to the other as the latter is to the whole line.*

Let AB be the line; it is required to divide it into two parts, Ax and xB, such that—

$$A x : x B : : x B : AB.$$

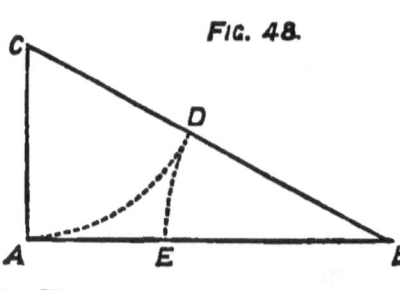

Fig. 48.

At A draw AC perpendicular to AB and equal·to half of it. Join CB. From C, with radius CA, describe an arc cutting CB in D. From B, with radius BD, describe an arc, cutting AB in E.

The point E divides AB as required; that is—

$$AE : EB : : EB : AB.$$

Problem 48.

182. *To produce a given line, so that the whole line, as produced, shall be to the given line as the latter is to the produced part.*

Let AB be the given line (fig. 49).

It is required to produce it by the additional line, BC, such that—

$$AC : AB : : AB : BC.$$

Bisect AB in D. Through B draw BE perpendicular

to AB and equal to it, and join DE. From the centre D, with the radius DE, describe an arc, meeting AB produced in C.

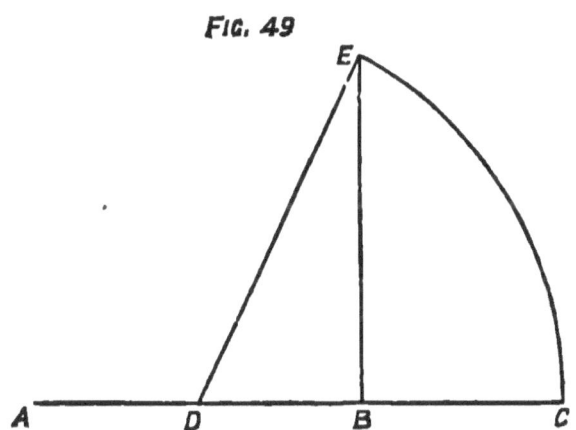

FIG. 49

C is the point to which AB must be produced to give the above proportion.

Problem 49.

183. *To divide a line in the same proportion as a given divided line.*

It is required to divide AB in the same proportion in which the line CD is divided.

Place AB parallel to CD at any convenient distance from it. Join AC and BD, and produce them till they meet in E, making a triangle AEB. From E draw lines through the points of division of CD, producing them to meet AB.

They will divide AB similarly to CD.

Elc. 50

184. *Note.*—As parallel lines cut diverging lines

proportionally; so, also, *diverging lines cut parallel lines in the same proportion.*

185. *Another method.*—Laying the point B on the point C, let AB and CD make any angle with each other, and join AD, making the triangle ABD (or ACD). Through the points of division of the line CD, draw lines parallel to AD. In the points in which these parallels cut AB, they will divide it in the same proportion as CD.

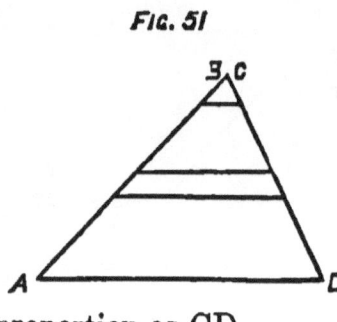

FIG. 51

Problem 50.

186. *To make a triangle similar to a given triangle.*

1. Make at the ends of any straight line two angles equal, each to each, to two angles of the given triangle. Producing the sides of these angles sufficiently, they will meet and form a triangle similar to the one given.

Note.—All the angles must be equal, for two of them are made equal; and as the whole angles of every triangle are equal to the same quantity (two right angles), the third angles also must be equal. And when two triangles are equiangular, it is a consequence that the sides about the equal angles are proportional.

187. 2. If the triangle is desired to be on a given line, which is to lie between two given angles, make angles equal to those at the end of the given line.

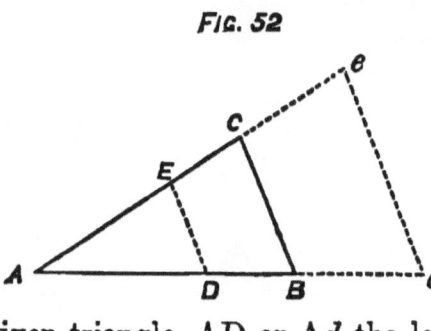

FIG. 52

Or, if ABC be the given triangle, AD or A*d* the length of the given line,

and A and B the angles, the equals of which are required at the ends of AD or A*d*.

Mark off in AB, or in AB produced, a part AD or *ad*
equal to the given line. Draw DE or *de* parallel to BC ;
in the latter case, producing AC to meet *de*.

The triangles ADE, A*de*, are each similar to the triangle ABC ; and have the given line AD or A*d*, between
angles equal to the two given angles, A and ABC.

188. *Note.*—The angles EDA, CBA, *ed*A are equal,
for—

*When a straight line, as A*d*, falls upon parallel lines,*
it makes the exterior angle equal to the interior opposite
on the same side ; that is, EDA to CBA ; CBA to *ed*A.

Problem 51.

189. *On a given straight line to construct a figure*
similar to a given rectilineal figure.

Let AB be the given line, and CDEFG the given figure.

FIG. 53

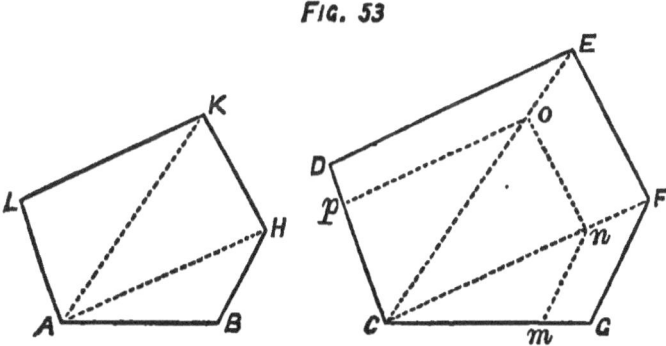

1. Divide the figure into triangles by the diagonals
CE, CF. On AB, make the triangle AHB similar to
CFG, angle B being equal to the angle G, and the
angle BAH equal to the angle FCG. On AH make
the triangle AKH, similar to the triangle CEF, placing
the right angles at the right ends of AH ; and on AK
make the triangle ALK similar to the triangle CDE.

The figure ALKHB, will be similar to the figure CDEFG.

2. Or, having drawn the diagonals CE, CF, take on CG, C*m* equal to AB. Through *m*, draw *mn* parallel to GF; through *n*, *no* parallel to FE; through *o*, *op* parallel to ED.

The figure C*ponm* is similar to the figure CDEFG, and on a line C*m*, equal to the given line AB.

If the required figure is to be on a line greater than CG, produce CG till equal to the given line, and having also produced CF and CE sufficiently, proceed as before.

Problem 52.

190. *To make a rectilineal figure similar to a given one, and having a given proportion to it.*

Let ABCD be the given figure, and AB : AE, the given proportion.

FIG. 54

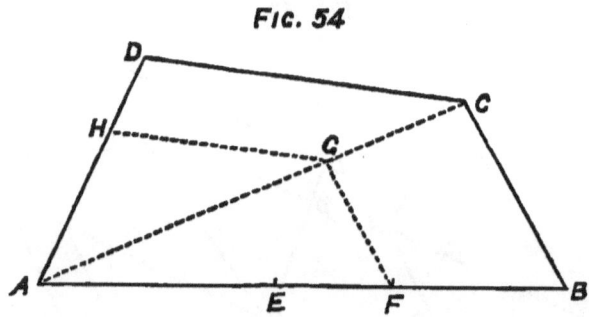

Find AF a mean proportional between AB and AE, (Problem 46). On AF make the figure AFGH similar to ABCD. Then—

ABCD : AFGH :: AB : AE.

DEFINITIONS—FOURTH SERIES.

Polygons.

191. A POLYGON is a plane figure contained by more than four straight lines.

192. A REGULAR POLYGON has all its sides equal, and all its angles equal. The rectilineal figure ABDEFG, page 63, is a regular polygon.

193. A regular polygon of five sides is called a *pentagon;* of six sides, a *hexagon;* of seven sides, a *heptagon;* of eight sides, an *octagon;* of nine sides, a *nonagon;* of ten sides, a *decagon.*

194. The CENTRE of a regular polygon is a point within, equidistant from the angular points. It is also equidistant from the sides.

195. The APOTHEM of a regular polygon is the perpendicular from the centre on any side.

196. A circle is said to be *inscribed in* a rectilineal figure, when every side touches the circle; that is, forms a tangent to the circle.

The rectilineal figure is then said to be *described about* the circle.

197. A circle is said to be *described about* a rectilineal figure, when its angular points are in the circumference of the circle. The rectilineal figure is then said to be *inscribed in* the circle.

Problem 53.

198. *To inscribe a circle within a triangle.*

Let ABC be the given triangle. Bisect any two angles, as A and B, by the lines AD, BD, meeting in the point D. D is equidistant from the sides of the triangle. From D draw DE perpendicular to any side, as AC.

A circle described from the centre D, with the radius

DE, will touch each side without cutting it, and will be
a circle inscribed in the triangle.

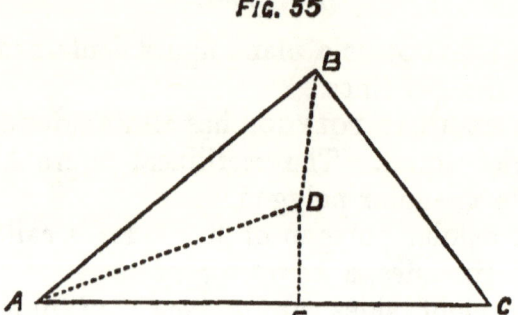

FIG. 55

199. *Note.*—This illustrates a property of the triangle
—*The straight lines bisecting the three angles of any triangle meet in one point, which is equidistant from the sides.*

To find that point, it is enough to bisect any two of
the angles.

Problem 54.

200. *To describe a circle about a triangle.*

This is, in reality, the same as Problem 37 ; to draw
a circle through three given points. See Note 2 to
that problem.

Problem 55.

FIG. 56

201. *To describe a circle
about a square.*

Let AEBD be the given
square. Draw the dia-
gonals intersecting in C.

A circle drawn from C
as centre, with the half
diagonal (CD) as radius,
will pass through the an-
gular points, forming a
circle described about the
square, AEBD.

Note.—*The diagonals of a square are equal and bisect each other ; the point of intersection being equidistant from the angular points.*

Problem 56.

202. *To inscribe a circle in a square.*
Let *mnop* be the given square : fig. 56.
Draw the diagonals, intersecting in C (they can be imagined). From C draw CD perpendicular to a side of the given square.
A circle drawn from the centre C, with the radius CD, will touch every side without cutting it, forming a circle inscribed in the square *mnop*.
Note.—The point of intersection of the diagonals of a square is equidistant from the sides.

Problem 57.

203. 1. *To inscribe a square in a circle, and* 2. *to describe a square about a circle.*
1. Draw two diameters, AB and DE, at right angles (fig. 56). Join their ends by the lines AE, EB, BD, DA ; these lines form a square inscribed in a circle.
204. 2. From the ends of two diameters at right angles, A, E, B, D, as centres, with the half diameter, CA, as radius, describes arcs on each side, cutting each other in the points *m, n, o, p.* Join *mn, no, op, pm.* The figure *mnop* will be a square described about the circle, each side touching the circle.
205. Or, draw tangents at the ends of two diameters at right angles, to be produced till they meet.
206. *Note* 1.—*To inscribe an octagon in a circle.* Bisect the arcs formed by two diameters at right angles. The points of bisection and ends of the diameters will be the angular points of the octagon.
207. *Note* 2.—The diagonals of a square intersect at right angles ; and each is equal to the side of the square

described about the circle in which the first square is
inscribed (AB or DE = mp or mn).

It is manifest also from the figure, that the square
of a line (mn) is equal to four times the square of half
the line (mA), and that a square is half the square of
its diagonal (DA² *half* of DE²).

The large square may be called the square of mn, or
of DE, which is equal to mn.

Problem 58.

208. 1. *To describe a circle about a regular polygon;
and,* 2. *to inscribe a circle in a regular polygon.*

1. Bisect two adjacent angles, A and B, by straight
lines meeting in the point C (fig. to next problem). This
point will be the centre of the polygon; and a circle
from C as centre, with the distance from C to any of the
angular points of the polygon as radius, will pass through
all its angular points, and form a circle described about
the polygon.

209. 2. From C, the centre of the polygon, found as
just described, draw a perpendicular on any side. A
circle from C as centre, with the perpendicular as radius,
will touch every side of the polygon, forming a circle
inscribed in the polygon.

Problem 59.

210. *To inscribe a regular polygon of any number of
sides in a given circle; also, to describe a polygon of a
like number of sides about a circle.*

Divide 360° by the given number of sides. This will
give the number of degrees of the central angle of the
polygon, ACB. Draw any radius, as CA. At C, in
the line CA, make the angle ACB equal to the central
angle just found, and join AB.

AB is a side of the required polygon. With AB as

radius, mark points round the circumference from A—G, F, E, D. The lines joining the adjacent points will form the required polygon.

FIG. 57

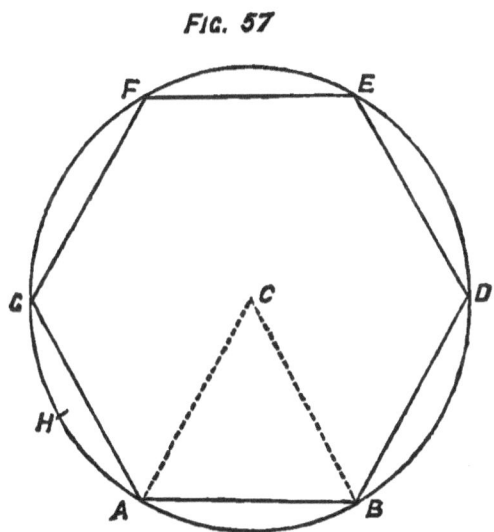

211. *Note.*—ACB is the *central angle of the polygon ;* that is, the angle at the centre opposite a side of the polygon. If *n* be the number of sides, the number of degrees in this angle is $\frac{360°}{n}$, that is the *n*th part of 360° ; or, the *n*th part of four right angles.

The angle at the circumference, as E, F, or GAB, is called the *angle of the polygon.* It is equal to the difference between the central angle and 180° ; or, $= 180° - \frac{360°}{n}$.

Each of the angles, CAG, CAB, is equal to *half the angle of the polygon ;* or, $= \frac{180° - (360° \div n)}{2}$.

212. A circumscribed polygon of the same number of sides may be formed by lines parallel to each side of

the inscribed polygon at the middle points of the arc it subtends ; or by tangents to the circle at the angular points of the inscribed polygon.

Problem 60.

213. *To describe a regular polygon on a given straight line.*

At each end of the given line, make an angle equal to half the angle of the polygon (Note, preceding problem) : the point where the sides of the angles meet will be the centre of the polygon. From that point as centre, with its distance to either end of the given line as radius, describe a circle. From one end of the given line, with it as radius, mark points round the circumference. The lines joining the adjacent points will form the required polygon.

Example.—If a pentagon, or five-sided regular polygon, be required on a given line, first, divide 360° by 5. This gives 72° as the central angle of the. polygon. Subtract 72° from 180°; this gives 108° as the angle of the polygon. The half of this, 54°, is the angle to be formed at each end of the given line.

Problem 61.

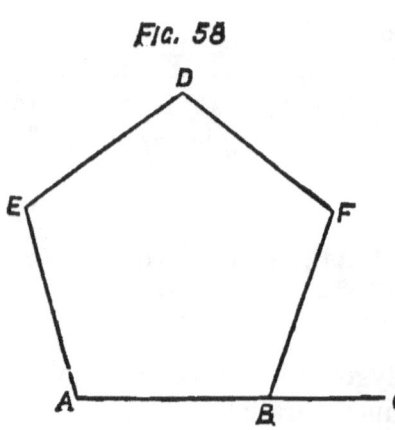

FIG. 58

214. *On a given straight line to construct a regular pentagon.*

Let AB be the straight line. Produce it to C, so that AC : AB :: AB : BC (Prob. 48). With AC as radius, from the centres A and B, describe arcs cutting each other in D. From A and D, with radius AB, describe arcs cutting in E ;

and from B and D, with the same radius, describe arcs cutting in F. Join AE, ED, DF, FB.

These, with AB, form a regular pentagon described on AB.

Problem 62.

215. *To make a regular hexagon on a given straight line.*

Let AB, fig. 57, be the given straight line. From A and B, with radius AB, describe arcs intersecting in C. With C as centre, and the same radius, describe a circle. It will pass through A and B. With the same radius, stepping round from A, mark the points G, F, E, D in the circumference. These, with A and B, will be angular points in the required polygon, which will be formed by straight lines joining the adjacent points.

216. *Note* 1.—The side of any hexagon is equal to the radius of the circumscribed circle. Hence—

To inscribe a hexagon in a circle.

With the radius of the circle, step round the circumference, marking six successive points. The lines joining these points will be a hexagon inscribed in the circle.

217. *Note* 2.—*To inscribe an equilateral triangle in a circle.* Mark, as just described, the points in the circumference for a hexagon. Lines joining alternate points will form an equilateral triangle inscribed in a circle ; as, AF, AD, FD, fig. 57.

218. *Note* 3.—*To inscribe a dodecagon* (a regular twelve-sided figure) *in a circle.* Mark, as in Note 1, two adjacent points in the circumference for a hexagon. Bisect the arc thus found, as AG in H, fig. 57.

The distance AH, applied to mark points round the circumference, will give the angular points of a dodecagon inscribed in the circle.

E

Problem 63.

219. *To make an octagon on a given straight line.*
Let AB be the given straight line.   Draw AC and

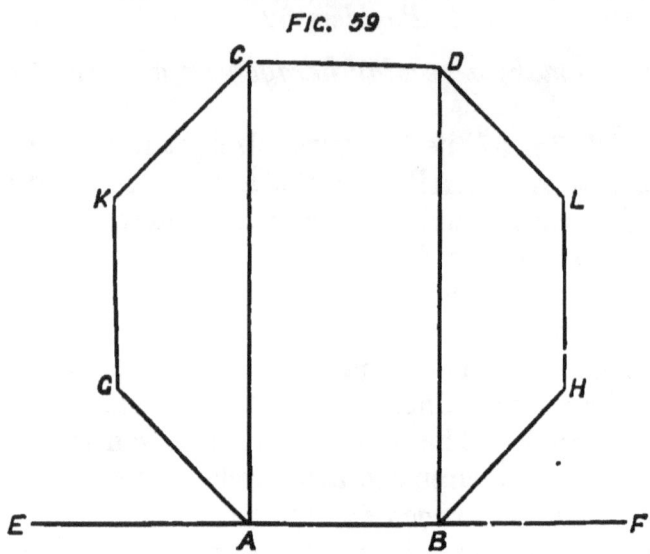

FIG. *59*

BD perpendicular to AB, and produce AB both ways,
to E and F.   Bisect the angles CAE and DBF by the
lines AG and BH, making each equal to AB.   Through
G and H, draw GK and HL parallel to AC or BD, and
each equal to AB.   From the centres K and L, with
the radius AB, cut AC in C and BD in D.   Join KC,
CD, DL.   ABHLDCKG is the required octagon.

EXERCISES ON SEVERAL OF THE PROBLEMS.

These exercises are designed to train to careful work,
and at the same time to interest and teach a few useful
geometrical truths.

220. *Problem 2.*—Draw any circle.   With the legs
of the compasses at the same distance used in drawing
it (*i.e.*, with the same radius), set one foot on any point

in the circumference, and with the other foot mark another point in the circumference. Keeping this last foot fixed, bring round the foot first set down, and mark a third point in the circumference ; and so on, stepping round with each foot alternately on a point in the circumference. The sixth step should bring the foot of the compasses back to the point first taken.

The circumference will thus be divided into six arcs of 60° each.

Join each point by straight lines to the points next it on each side. Each line thus drawn will be the chord of 60°.

It is thus plain that, in every circle, the chord of 60° is equal to the radius.

The rectilineal figure formed by these six chords is a regular hexagon, or regular six-sided figure.

221. Draw a circle. From any point in the circumference, with the same radius, draw an arc within the circle, its ends being in the circumference. Step round the circle, drawing similar arcs from the ends of those previously described, till six such arcs have been drawn.

If correctly done, these arcs will all pass through the centre, and their twelve ends will meet, two and two, in six points in the circumference, dividing it into six arcs of 60° each. Carefully done, this forms a very elegant figure.

222. *Problem* 3.—Find three or more points, each equidistant from the ends of any straight line. Join the equidistant points. If correctly done, they will be in the same straight line ; and that line, sufficiently produced, will bisect the given straight line, and be at right angles to it.

This illustrates a geometrical truth, already pointed out (70).

223. *Problem* 4.—Bisect each of the angles of any

triangle : the bisecting lines should intersect each other in the same point.

224. Draw any two straight lines cutting each other. Bisect each of the four angles at the point of intersection. Each bisecting line should be at right angles to the adjacent bisecting lines, and continuous with the opposite one.

225. Bisect the angle between the equal sides of an isosceles triangle, or any angle of an equilateral triangle. The bisecting line will bisect the base, and be at right angles to it. See Note 2, Problem 4. If DE be drawn, BDE is an isosceles or equilateral triangle.

226. *Problem 5.*—If the operation has been accurately done, the bisecting line, CD, will be at right angles to the line to be bisected, AB.

227. Bisect the base of an isosceles triangle, or any side of an equilateral triangle. The straight line from the point of bisection to the opposite angle will bisect that angle, and be at right angles to the side bisected.

228. Bisect any two sides of a triangle. The line joining the points of bisection will be parallel to the third side, and equal to half of it.

229. Bisect the four sides of any quadrilateral. The line joining the points of bisection of the adjacent sides will form a parallelogram.

230. *Problems 6, 7.*—Bisect the base of an isosceles triangle, or any side of an equilateral triangle. Through the point of bisection, draw inwards a perpendicular to the bisected line. The perpendicular will pass through the opposite angular point and bisect the angle there.

231. Bisect any straight line. From the point of bisection, draw a perpendicular both ways. Every point of this perpendicular should be equidistant from the ends of the line.

232. Bisect any angle. From any point in the bisecting line, draw perpendiculars to the sides. They should be equal.

Note.—The straight line bisecting an angle is the *locus* of points equidistant from its sides ; that is, any point equidistant from the sides is in that line.

233. From the angular points of any triangle, draw perpendiculars to the opposite sides. They should meet in one point, within the triangle, or without it when produced.

234. Bisect the sides of any triangle. At the points of bisection, draw perpendiculars. They will meet in one point, which will be equidistant from the angular points of the triangle. If the triangle is acute angled, the perpendiculars will meet within it ; if right angled, in the middle point of the hypotenuse ; if obtuse angled, without the triangle.

235. Bisect the three angles of a triangle. From the point in which the bisecting lines meet, draw perpendiculars to the sides. These perpendiculars should be equal, and a circle from their point of intersection as centre, with one of them as radius, should pass through the ends of all the perpendiculars, and touch each side without cutting it.

236. *Problem* 8.—Let ABC be any angle less than a right angle. At C, on the same side of BC, make an angle equal to ABC, with its other side leaning towards BA. The sides of the two equal angles will meet, if produced sufficiently, and an isosceles triangle will be formed, the sides opposite the equal angles being equal.

Next, make the angle at C equal to ABC to lie the other way, producing BC. The side of the angle at C will now be parallel to BA ; illustrating the geometrical truth mentioned in Par. 188.

237. *Problem* 9.—Trisect any right angle, ABE, by the lines BC, next to BA, and BD next to BE. At A and E, in the lines AB, EB, make angles, each equal to ABD or CBE ; that is, two-thirds of a right angle. Let the trisecting lines be sufficiently produced to meet the

sides of the latter angles.   Two equilateral triangles will
be formed, each divided into two right-angled triangles.

238. *Problem* 14.—Having bisected any side of a
triangle, through the point of bisection draw straight
lines parallel to the other sides.   These lines bisect the
sides which they cut.   The line joining the points of
bisection of the latter sides is parallel to the side first
bisected.   The whole triangle is divided into four triangles, equal in all respects, and equiangular with the
large triangle.   Also, three different parallelograms are
formed within the original triangle.

239. Draw any two parallel lines, and then two other
parallel lines crossing them.   A parallelogram will be
formed, exhibiting the following properties :—
The opposite sides parallel.
The opposite sides equal.
The opposite angles equal.
The diagonals bisecting one another.

240. *Problem* 15.—Take any triangle having no two
sides equal.   On the other side of any side of it, make
another triangle having its sides equal, each to each, to
the sides of the first triangle.   In the quadrilateral
formed, place the equal sides opposite, not adjacent to
each other.   The figure should be a parallelogram.

241. Do the same, except in placing the equal sides
adjacent, not opposite.   The straight line joining the
vertices of the two triangles will cut the common side,
or that side produced, at right angles, and will be
bisected by it.

242. *Problem* 17.—Make a rectangle, of which the
adjacent sides are 3 and 4 of any convenient measure
of length ; or, any multiples of these numbers.   The
diagonal should be 5, or the same multiple of 5 ; and
the two diagonals should be equal and should bisect
each other.   If 9 and 12 be taken as the lengths of the
adjacent sides, the diagonal should be 15, and so on.

243. Make a square. Square the number representing the length of the side; the square root of double the number thus produced will give the length of the diagonal, if the figure be correctly drawn.

244. Draw squares and rectangles, and test their accuracy by the following properties :—The diagonals of each should be equal, and should bisect each other : the opposite sides should be equal. Produce each side both ways. The outer angles thus produced should be right angles.

245. *Problem* 20.—Draw any right-angled triangle, and describe a square on the hypotenuse. Produce either side of the triangle at the point where it meets the hypotenuse, and make the part produced equal to the other side of the triangle. On the whole line thus formed make a square, including the triangle. If correctly drawn, the sides of this square will pass through the angular points of the first formed square, and will contain exactly the inner square, the first formed triangle, and three other triangles equal to it in all respects.

246. Draw any square or rhombus. The diagonals should bisect the angles, and bisect each other at right angles.

INTRODUCTION TO ALGEBRA.

247. Algebra is a kind of arithmetic, in which the letters of the alphabet, as well as figures, are employed to represent numbers, and the relations between them are expressed by certain characters called *signs*.

248. The following terms, having the same meanings as in arithmetic, are much used in Algebra. With these meanings, the learner must be perfectly familiar.

The *sum* of two or more quantities is the quantity procured by adding them.   49 is the sum of 4, 13, and 32.

The *difference* of two quantities is the quantity procured by subtracting the less from the greater.   17 is the difference of 49 and 32.

The *product* of several quantities is the quantity procured by multiplying them together.   22 is the product of 11, 4, and $\frac{1}{2}$.

The *factors* of a quantity or of a product are any quantities which, multiplied by one another, produce it. 8, 3, and 1 are factors of 24 ; 12 and 3 are factors of 36 ; also, 9 and 4 ; 6 and 6 ; 36 and 1 ; 2, 3, 6.

A *dividend* is a quantity to be divided ; a *divisor* is a quantity by which we divide ; the *quotient* denotes how often the divisor is contained in the dividend— also, the divisor*th* * part of the dividend ; the *remainder* is what is over in division—that is, the difference between the dividend and divisor times * the quotient.

In dividing 48 by 5, 48 is the dividend, 5 the divisor, and 9 the quotient—denoting that 48 contains 5 nine times—and 3 is the remainder ; that is, the difference between 48 and 5 times 9.

Carrying out the division more completely, $9\frac{3}{5}$ is the complete quotient—denoting that 48 contains 5, $9\frac{3}{5}$ times ; also, that $9\frac{3}{5}$ is the exact 5th part of 48.   The dividend, 48, is separated into two parts, 45 and 3 ; 9 is the 5th part of 45 ; $\frac{3}{5}$ is the 5th part of 3.

Algebraic Signs.

249. Sign of Equality.—The sign =, read *equal to*, denotes that the quantities between which it is placed are exactly equal to one another.

---

* Such expressions are extremely convenient.   Their use would greatly simplify arithmetical language and explanations.   We use *th* and *times* freely with numbers ; they can be used also advantageously with words, or letters which represent numbers.

250. SIGN OF ADDITION. — The sign +, read *plus*, means that the quantity to which it is prefixed is to be added.

Examples.—The expression 4 + 5, denotes that 5 is to be added to 4 ; meaning, therefore, 9, or the sum of 4 and 5. So, $a + b$ denotes that b is to be added to a. If a stands for 8, and b for 9, then the value of $a + b$ is 17. There may be several quantities, as $a + b + c$. The expression $4 + 7 = 3 + 8$, means that the sum of 4 and 7 is equal to the sum of 3 and 8. In like manner, we may have $a + b = x + y$; or, $a + 7 = x + 3$.

251. SIGN OF SUBTRACTION. — The sign −, read *minus* (or, *less by*), means that the quantity before which it is placed is to be subtracted.

Examples.—The expression 11 − 4, means that 4 is to be subtracted from 11, and is equivalent to 7, the difference of these two numbers. The expression $a − b$, denotes that b is to be subtracted from a. $4 + 9 = 18 − 5$, denotes that when we add 4 to 9, the result is the same as when we subtract 5 from 18.

252. Quantities with the sign + prefixed are called *positive ;* those with the sign − prefixed are called *negative*.

253. When no sign is prefixed, which is usual with the quantity at the extreme left, the quantity is regarded as *positive*, the sign + being understood ; and we must deal with it as if + were prefixed to it. So $a − b$, means $+ a − b$.

254. SIGN OF MULTIPLICATION.—The sign ×, read *multiplied by* (or, *times*), means that the quantities between which it is placed are to be multiplied, the one by the other ; the whole expresses their product. $7 × 9$, means 7 times 9, or 9 times 7, or 7 multiplied by 9 ; and denotes their product, 63. Also, $a × b$, means a times b, or b taken as often as there are units in a ; or b times a (a taken as often as there are units in b) ; for a times b and b times a are the same.

255. But, in algebra, this sign is more usually omitted ; *multiplication being understood when the letters, or numbers and letters, are simply placed side by side.* In short, in algebra, we denote the product of any factors by setting them side by side.

Examples.—3a means—

3 multiplied by *a*,
a multiplied by 3,
3 times *a*, or
a times 3 ;

all of which denote the same, the product of 3 and *a*. So, *ab* means the product of *a* and *b* ; that is, *a* times *b*, or *b* times *a*. There is no difference between *ab* and *a* × *b* ; the latter is a form seldom used.

256. The expression 3*abc*, means the product of 3, *a*, *b*, and *c*. If *a* stands for 4, *b* for 5, *c* for 6, then 3*abc* means the same as 3 × 4 × 5 × 6, or 360.

257. The order in which the factors of a product are placed is immaterial. Thus,

$$3 \times 4 \times 7 = 4 \times 3 \times 7 = 7 \times 3 \times 4 = 84 ;$$

and *ac* means the same as *ca*.

258. SIGN OF DIVISION.—The sign ÷ , read *divided by,* denotes that the quantity after which it is placed is to be divided by that to which the sign is prefixed. Thus, 14 ÷ 2, means 14 divided by 2.

259. But the most usual way of expressing division in algebra is, by placing the dividend *above,* and the divisor *below,* with a line between, in the form of a fraction. The whole expresses the quotient got by dividing the upper quantity by the lower : the line meaning *divided by.* Shortly, a fraction means—the *denominatorth* part of the *numerator.**

Examples.—$\frac{16}{4}$ denotes 4, or the quotient of the divi-

---

* The upper quantity is called the numerator ; the lower one, the denominator.

sion of 16 by 4; that is, 16 divided by 4, or the 4th part of 16. So, $\dfrac{a+b}{c}$ denotes the quotient of the division of $a+b$ by c. If a be 34, b 6, c 8, then $\dfrac{a+b}{c}$ denotes 5; and the value of $\dfrac{a-b}{c-4}$ is 7.

260. SIGN OF INVOLUTION.—This is a small numeral or letter placed a little above and at the right of the quantity to which it belongs; and denotes a *certain power of that quantity.*

261. A power of a quantity means *the quantity itself, or its product by itself a certain number of times.*

262. The sign of involution attached to a quantity is called its *index* or *exponent.*

In multiplying 4 once by 4 (4×4), 4 is taken twice as a factor. The product may be written 4^2, and is then called the *second power* or *square* of 4. The small 2 is the index or exponent of the second power of any quantity.

When 4 is taken thrice as a factor ($4 \times 4 \times 4$), the product may be written 4^3, and is then called the *third power* or *cube* of 4; and a small 3 is the index of that power.

263. The quantity itself is considered its *first* power, its index as such being 1. Thus 4^1 is the same as 4. This index is seldom written, being usually omitted as understood. Sometimes it has to be reckoned, and added to or subtracted from other indices.

$4^1 = 4$; $4^2 = 16$; $4^3 = 64$; $4^4 = 256$; $4^5 = 1024$.

The last is the fifth power of 4.

264. Thus, in involution, the quantity is to be multiplied by itself *once less* than the number of times denoted by its index, which expresses the number of times the quantity is taken as a factor. To get 4^3, we multiply 4 *twice* by itself, or write it *thrice* as a factor ($4 \times 4 \times 4$).

265. So, instead of writing aa, we write a^2, meaning a multiplied once by itself ; for aaa, we write a^3, meaning a multiplied twice by itself. The first power of a is a^1, or, simply, a.

This is called *involution*, or raising a quantity to one of its powers.

266. SIGN OF EVOLUTION, or *radical sign.*—The sign $\sqrt{}$, together with the quantity before which it is placed, denotes some *root* of that quantity. A root is a quantity, one of whose powers is the quantity to which the radical sign is prefixed.

267. The sign $\sqrt{}$, or $\sqrt[2]{}$, denotes the *square root,* that root whose square (or second power) is the quantity before which it is placed.

Examples.—The expression $\sqrt{9}$, called *the square root of* 9, means 3, or that quantity whose square is 9. The square of 3, or 3^2, is 9. So, $\sqrt{a}$ is that quantity whose square is a. $\sqrt{a} \times \sqrt{a} = a$. The square root of a^2, or $\sqrt{a^2}$, is that quantity whose square is a^2; that is, a; for $aa = a^2$.

The sign $\sqrt[3]{}$, denotes the *third root*, or *cube root;* that root whose cube is the quantity before which it is placed.

Examples.—The $\sqrt[3]{125}$ is 5, for 5^3, that is, $5 \times 5 \times 5$, $= 125$. $\sqrt[3]{b^3}$ is b, for b, raised to the third power, is b^3.

268. Roots are sometimes expressed by *fractional indices.* Then, the upper number denotes the power, the lower figure the root. Thus, $a^{\frac{1}{2}}$ is the same as $\sqrt{a}$, meaning the square root of the first power of a; $a^{\frac{1}{3}}$ is the cube root of a; $a^{\frac{2}{3}}$ is the same as $\sqrt[3]{a^2}$, meaning the cube root of a^2.

269. CO-EFFICIENTS.—The number prefixed as a factor to any quantity is called its co-efficient.

Examples.—In the expressions $3a$, $7bc$, $\frac{1}{4}d$, the numbers 3, 7, $\frac{1}{4}$ are co-efficients.

270. When no co-efficient is expressed, the co-efficient

1 is understood, and has sometimes to be reckoned : 1a is the same as a.

271. The co-efficient is a multiplier, and shows how often the quantity following it is to be taken. Thus 8xy means 8 times the quantity xy.

272. Letters may sometimes be considered as co-efficients. In the expressions ab, cd^2, 5xy, a, c, 5x may be considered as co-efficients, meaning a times b, c times d^2, 5x times y.

273. Algebraic expressions may often be simplified by adding or subtracting co-efficients of the same quantity. Thus 5a + 7a may be condensed into one term, (5 + 7) a, or 12a : so 13b - 6b can be reduced to one term, (13 - 6) b, or 7b.

In like manner, ax + bx may be brought to one term, (a + b) x ; cy - dy may be expressed as (c - d) y.

Ratio—Proportion.

274. A *Ratio* is the relation of one quantity to another of the same kind, in respect to their magnitude.

The relation of 2 to 3, in regard to their magnitude, is this :—2 is, or contains, 2 times the third part of 3 ; that is, 2 is 2 times 1, and 3 is 3 times 1. Expressed fractionally, 2 is $\frac{2}{3}$ of 3.

The ratio of 2 to 3 is therefore said to be $\frac{2}{3}$, or 2 : 3 ; for ratio is expressed both ways.

In like manner, the ratio of 3 to 2 is 3 : 2 ; $\frac{3}{2}$; or 1$\frac{1}{2}$; for $\frac{3}{2}$ is the same as 1$\frac{1}{2}$. We see at once that 3 is one and a half of 2.

275. As $\frac{2}{3}$ is the same as 2 divided by 3, and $\frac{3}{2}$ the same as 3 divided by 2, the upper number being *divi-dend*, the lower, *divisor ; the ratio of one number to another is found by dividing the former by the latter.* That operation shows how often the first contains the second.

Examples.—Find the ratio of 12 to 4.   12 ÷ 4, or
$\frac{12}{4} = 3$.   It is manifest that 12 contains 4 three times.

Find the ratio of 11 : 4.   11 ÷ 4, or $\frac{11}{4}$, $= 2\frac{3}{4}$.   11 contains 2 times 4 and $\frac{3}{4}$ of 4,—the ratio required is therefore 11 : 4, $\frac{11}{4}$, or $2\frac{3}{4}$.

Find the ration of 9 to 12. $\frac{9}{12}$, brought to lowest
terms, is $\frac{3}{4}$.   The ratio required is therefore 3 : 4, or $\frac{3}{4}$.
And it is plain that 9 contains 3 times the 4th part of
12.

276. The first term of a ratio is called the *antecedent*
(or, going before term) ; the second term, the *consequent*
(or, following term).

277. A *proportion* is formed by the terms of two
equal ratios, properly arranged.

The ratio of 2 to 7 is equal to that of 6 to 21 ; for
$\frac{2}{7}$ are equal to $\frac{6}{21}$.   These numbers, then, form a proportion, the numerators being the *antecedents* of the two
ratios, while the denominators are the *consequents*.   This
proportion is written—

$$2 : 7 :: 6 : 21, \text{ or}$$
$$2 : 7 = 6 : 21,$$

and is usually expressed, 2 *is to* 7 *as* 6 *is to* 21 ; that
is, 2 has the same proportion to 6 as 7 has to 21 ;
which is manifest, each antecedent being $\frac{2}{7}$ of its consequent.

Similarly, if $\frac{a}{b} = \frac{c}{d}$, then these four quantities form a
a proportion,

$$\text{and } a : b :: c : d.$$

If four lines, A, B, C, D, are of such magnitude that
the ratio of A to B is equal to that of C to D, these
lines form a proportion,

$$\text{and } A : B :: C : D.$$

If the length of A were such that it contained one and
a quarter of B, then C would contain one and a quarter
of D.

Quantities which form a proportion are often said to be *proportional*.

278. A *fourth proportional* to three quantities, is a quantity which with them forms a proportion; that is, *two equal ratios*. Thus 10 is a fourth proportional to 2, 4, and 5, for

$$2 : 4 :: 5 : 10.$$

In the Rule of Three, we find a fourth proportional to three given terms.

279. A *third proportional* to two quantities, is a quantity such that one of the given quantities is to the other as the latter is to the third proportional. Thus 25 is a third proportional to 4 and 10, for

$$4 : 10 :: 10 : 25.$$

280. A *mean proportional* between two quantities, is a quantity such that one quantity is to the mean proportional as the latter is to the other quantity. 10 is a mean proportional between 4 and 25.

281. When four quantities form a proportion, the product of the 1st and 4th is equal to the product of the 2d and 3d; or, as usually expressed, *the product of the extremes is equal to the product of the means*. The 1st and 4th are the *extremes;* the 2d and 3d are the *means.*

If $a : b :: c : d$, then $ad = bc$.

If $3 : 8 :: 2 : 5\frac{1}{3}$, then $3 \times 5\frac{1}{3} = 8 \times 2 = 16$.

Also, the quotient of the first by either of the means, is equal to the quotient of the other mean by the fourth.

If $4 : 10 :: 6 : 15$,

then $\frac{4}{10} = \frac{6}{15}$; and $\frac{4}{6} = \frac{10}{15}$.

THE EQUATION.

282. The Equation is an algebraic expression, denoting the equality of two quantities. It is very useful for exhibiting, in a compendious form, *rules* or *formulæ*

for finding some unknown quantity, from certain other quantities, known or given.

283. In algebra, unknown quantities are usually represented by the last letters of the alphabet, x, y, z; known quantities by the first letters, a, b, c, &c.

284. On the *left* of the equation is placed a letter standing for the unknown number or quantity required to be found; on the *right* are set the quantities which must be known to find the quantity sought, with *signs*, indicating what must be done with them; and the sign of equality ($=$) is placed between, denoting that the quantity at the left is equal to the quantity at the right; that is, equal to the result obtained by performing the operations indicated on the quantities at the right.

285. The following is an equation :—

$$x = \frac{36 - 4}{2}.$$

Let the number to be found be denoted by the letter x; then x is equal to the result obtained by performing the operations indicated at the right. That is, translating the above equation or formula into ordinary language, it may be read thus—

To find the value of x, subtract 4 from 36, and divide the difference by 2—

Whence, $x = 16.$

In like manner, the equation,

$$x = \frac{ab}{c} + d,$$

translated, means—

To find x, multiply a by b, divide the product by c, and to the quotient add d.

286. In the following equation, referring to a question in interest—

$$I = \frac{PRY}{100},$$

let P stand for a sum of money lent, called *the principal ;*
R for the *rate per cent. per annum* (interest of £100 for
1 year); Y for the *time* during which the money is
lent, *expressed in years;* and I for the interest of the
sum P, at the rate R, and for the time Y.

Then, the above equation expresses very shortly a
most useful rule, namely—

To find the interest of a sum of money, multiply the
sum (or principal) by the rate per cent. per annum, that
product by the time expressed in years, and divide the
last product by 100.*

287. It is an advantage of the equation that from it
rules or formulæ may easily be framed to find any of
the quantities named that may happen to be the unknown one.

From the preceding equation,

$$I = \frac{PRY}{100},$$

we may form other equations, expressing the rule to find
P, R, or Y, should any of these be the unknown quantity, the others and I being known.

288. This is done by a series of operations, the object
of which is to separate the quantity sought from all the
other quantities, and get it on one side of the equation
by itself, as I is in the above equation. Step by step
the other quantities are disengaged from the unknown
one, and carried to the other side of the mark =, leaving
the quantity unknown standing alone on one side.

289. In clearing off these quantities, we must ever
keep both sides of the equation equal. To secure this,
we must always do the same to both sides. The two

---

* Decimals are taught so little, or so late, in this country, that
the simpler rule of multiplying P by the years, and by the interest
of £1 for one year at the given rate, expressed decimally, is not
much used, and the above is better known. It is also fully better
suited for the purpose on hand.

F

sides will then continue equal, just as, if to the two scales of a balance equally poised, we add equal weights, or if we take out equal weights, they will still remain equally poised. We must add the same quantity to both sides of the equation, or subtract the same quantity from both sides, multiply both sides by the same number, or divide both sides by the same number, &c.

Quantities in an equation are disengaged from any quantity we may wish to place by itself on one side by the following operations :—

290. 1. To clear off a multiplier from the unknown quantity, *divide every term on both sides by that multiplier.*

Example.—If— $3x = 60.$

Here x is encumbered with 3 as a multiplier. Dividing both sides of the equation by 3, we get the· new equation, $x = 20.$

291. 2. To clear off a divisor, *multiply both sides of the equation by that divisor.*

Example.—If— $\dfrac{4x}{3} = 14.$

Here x is encumbered with 3 as a divisor. We first clear it off by multiplying both sides of the equation by 3. This gives the equation,

$$4x = 42.$$

We then clear off the 4 as the 3 was cleared off from the first equation, and thus find that—

$$x = 10\tfrac{1}{2}.$$

If— $\dfrac{x}{a} = c,$

we must clear off the divisor a, by multiplying both sides by it. This gives—

$$x = ac.$$

Every term on both sides must be multiplied by the

divisor we wish to clear off, or divided by the multi-plier we desire to get rid of.

292. Multiplying by the divisors clears off fractions, the denominators of which are *divisors*. If there be several fractions, multiply at once by a common multiple of all the denominators;—best, by their least common multiple.

If—
$$\frac{x}{2} + \frac{3x}{5} = 12.$$

Multiply both sides by 10, the least common multiple of 2 and 5.

This gives—
$$\frac{10x}{2} + \frac{30x}{5} = 120;$$
$$\text{or, } 5x + 6x = 120;$$
$$\text{or, } 11x = 120;$$
$$\text{or, } x = 10\tfrac{10}{11}.$$

293. 3. To clear off a quantity *added*, *subtract* it from both sides.

4. To clear off a quantity *subtracted*, *add* it to both sides.

The two last rules are more shortly expressed—

3, 4. Clear off a quantity with + or − before it, by carrying it to the other side and changing its sign.

This is called *transposing*, and is the same in effect as subtracting the quantity from both sides, or adding it to both sides.

If—
$$x + 5 = 11,$$
transpose the 5, which will give—
$$x = 11 - 5.$$

Here, 5 has been subtracted from both sides.

If—
$$x - 7 = 8,$$
transpose the 7, which will give—
$$x = 8 + 7.$$

Here, 7 has been added to both sides; to the left side, as that side at first expressed x less 7 ; and now expressing x, denotes 7 more than at first; or, has had 7 added to it.

$$\text{If—} \qquad 3x - 10 = 2x + 5,$$

transpose 10 and $2x$; then,

$$3x - 2x = 10 + 5;$$
$$\text{or, } x = 15.$$

294. 5. If the unknown quantity is a root, get it by itself on one side, and raise both sides to the corresponding power.

$$\text{If—} \qquad \sqrt{x} + 3 = 10,$$

transpose the 3, which will give—

$$\sqrt{x} = 10 - 3; \text{ or, } \sqrt{x} = 7.$$

Then square both sides, which will clear off the radical sign from x, and we find, $x = 49$.

295. 6. If the unknown quantity is a power, get it by itself on one side, and extract the corresponding root of both sides.

$$\text{If—} \qquad x^2 - 20 = 44,$$

transpose the 20, which gives—

$$x^2 = 64.$$

Extract the square root of both sides; then we have—

$$x = 8.$$

296. Thus, whatever operation any quantity in an equation performs on the unknown quantity, we must perform the *reverse operation* on the whole, to remove the former from the unknown quantity. To remove a *multiplier*, divide by it, &c.

297. Having then the equation,

$$I = \frac{PRY}{100},$$

as the rule to find the interest, when we know principal, rate, and time, we can extract from this a rule or formula to find the principal or P, when it is unknown, and I, R, and Y are known. We must disengage R, Y, and 100 from P, and get it by itself on one side of a new equation.

298. 1. Remove the divisor 100 by multiplying both sides by 100. This gives—

$$I \times 100 = PRY.$$

To multiply a fraction by the denominator, we simply cancel the denominator.

299. 2. We next remove from P the multipliers RY, by dividing both sides by RY. This gives—

$$\frac{I \times 100}{RY} = P.$$

PRY ÷ RY gives P; for when we divide a product by the product of any of its factors, the result or answer is—the other factors.

300. At each step an equation was still formed, for the same thing was done to both sides.

The unknown term is now by itself on one side; on the other side are the known terms, with signs denoting what to do with them to get the quantity sought.

301. Thus, from the formula for finding interest, a rule to find the principal has easily been extracted—namely,

To find the principal which will yield a given interest at a given rate, and given time expressed in years,—multiply the interest by 100, and divide that product by the rate and by the years.

302. In like manner, from this last, or from the original equation, we may form an equation expressing the formula to find R, or that for Y.

303. Similarly, also, from other equations we may extract equations showing the values of, or formulæ for finding any quantities they contain.

304. If the unknown quantity is one of the terms of a proportion, an equation is easily formed, from which its value can be found.

When four quantities are proportional, the product of the extremes (first and last terms) is always equal to the product of the means (the two middle terms).

Thus, 4 : 7 :: 12 : 21 ;

and accordingly we find that—

$$4 \times 21 = 7 \times 12,$$

the product in each case being 84.

In like manner, if—

$$a : b :: c : d, \text{ then}$$
$$ad = bc.$$

305. From this equation, by division, the value of any of the four quantities may be found.

If the fourth term in the proportion, d, is the unknown quantity, then, dividing both sides of the equation by a, to clear off a as a multiplier of d, we have the formula,

$$d = \frac{bc}{a}.$$

This example, it is manifest, is the common Rule of Three, where, from three terms given, we find a fourth : —Divide the product of the second and third terms by the first term.

306. In the same manner, equations may be formed to express the rule for finding any other of the four terms in a proportion—always understanding that they are arranged in proper order, so that the first is to the second as the third is to the fourth.

307. It is not necessary to form the equation : its result may be found by simple inspection of the proportion. If one *extreme* is the quantity sought, the other *extreme* is the divisor, and the product of the *means* is the dividend ; if one of the *means* is the unknown quantity, the other *mean* is the divisor, the product of the *extremes* the dividend.

Examples and Exercises.

308. When two forces act on a lever, there is equilibrium (they balance each other), if one force (F) is to the other force (f) as the perpendicular from the fulcrum on the direction of the second force (p), is to the perpendicular from the fulcrum on the direction of the first force (P) ; that is, when

$$F : f :: p :. P.$$

Extract the formulæ, or equational rules for finding each of these four quantities.

309. When several terms on one side of an equation consist of the same kind of quantity, they are to be *collected* into one term. Thus $6x + x$ are the same as $7x$; $8x - 3x$ (8 times x less 3 times x) are to be collected into one term, $5x$.

Examples.

If from the equation,

$$2x + \frac{x}{3} = 28,$$

we wish to find the value of x ; multiplying by 3 to get rid of the fraction,

$$6x + x = 84;$$

Collecting, $\qquad 7x = 84$;

Dividing by 7, $\qquad x = 12.$

If from the equation,

$$x = abc + d,$$

we wish to find the formula for c, we must get c by itself on one side.

Transposing d, $\quad x - d = abc$;

Dividing by ab, $\quad \dfrac{x - d}{ab} = c.$

If $x^2 + 7 = 56$, find x.

Transposing 7, . . $\quad x^2 = 56 - 7$;

Collecting, . . $\quad x^2 = 49$;

Extracting the square root, $x = 7.$

$Ex.$—1. $x+13=40$, . . . $Ans.$—$x=27$.

2. $x-13=40$, . . . $x=53$.

3. $2x=x+10$, . . . $x=10$.

4. $2x-10=20$, . . . $x=15$.

5. $3x=x+14$, . . . $x=7$.

6. $2x+16=3x$, . . . $x=16$.

7. $x-a=b$, . . . $x=b+a$.

8. $3x-6=34-x$, . . . $x=10$.

9. $4xy=2a$ . . . $x=\dfrac{a}{2y}$.

10. $x+\dfrac{x}{2}=150-6x$, . . $x=20$.

11. $x+\dfrac{x}{2}+\dfrac{x}{3}=11$, . . . $x=6$.

12. $20-3x-8=60-7x$, . . $x=12$.

13. $2x-\dfrac{x}{2}+1=5x-2$, . . $x=-\dfrac{6}{7}$.

14. $3x-5=23-x$, . . . $x=7$.

15. $x+\dfrac{x}{2}-\dfrac{x}{3}=4x-17$, . . $x=6$.

16. $\sqrt{x}=7$, . . . $x=49$.

17. $\sqrt{x}-3=7$, . . . $x=100$.

18. $\sqrt[3]{x}=5$, . . . $x=125$.

19. $x^2+21=70$, . . $x=7$.

20. $x^2-30=70$, . . $x=10$.

21. $3x^2+16=116-x^2$, . . $x=5$.

22. $x^3+9=1009$, . . $x=10$.

23. $x+2=\dfrac{5x}{6}+4$, . . . $x=12$.

24. $\dfrac{2x}{5}-7=1$, . . . $x=20$.

25. $x+6:x::3:2$, . . $x=12$.

26. $7x^2-19=324$, . . . $x=7$.

27. $\dfrac{3x^2+7}{10}=37$, . . . $x=11$.

28. $x+\dfrac{x}{4}-\dfrac{x}{5}=10\frac{1}{2}$, . . . $x=10$.

29. $\dfrac{x}{3}+\dfrac{x}{4}-7=0$, . . . $x=12$.

30. $3x+c=a+b$, . . . $x=\dfrac{a+b-c}{3}$.

310. When the pupil feels embarrassed by the sign −
prefixed to x towards the close of the working of an
equation, he may change the signs of all the terms on
both sides; the two sides will continue equal.

INTRODUCTION TO MENSURATION.

311. Mensuration is the art of measuring the lengths
of lines, areas of surfaces, and volumes (or capacities)
of solids or spaces.

312. *Measures of Length.*

Inches.	Feet.		Yards.		Poles.		Furlongs.		Mile.
1 =	·083								
12 =	1								
36 =	3	=	1						
198 =	16½	=	5½	=	1				
7920 =	660	=	220	=	40	=	1		
63360 =	5280	=	1760	=	·320	=	8	=	1

The inch is divided into *eighths* or into *twelfths*, or
decimally into *tenths*.

In land-surveying a chain is used. Its length is 4 poles
—that is, 22 yards, 66 feet, or 792 inches. It consists
of 100 links, each of which is 7·92, or 7$\frac{23}{25}$ inches long.

313. *Metric System.*—The length of the French
standard, the *metre*, is 3·28089 feet, or 39·37079
inches. The *kilometre* (1000 metres) is 1093·633
yards—very nearly 1093$\frac{2}{3}$ yards. The decimetre (tenth
of a metre) is 3·937 inches.

The English foot is 3·0479 decimetres; the yard,
0·91438 metre; the mile, 1609·3149 metres.

314. The mean length of a degree of latitude is
69·0444 miles. A nautical or geographical mile is the
60th part of this, or 6075·6 feet.

The length of a degree of longitude at the equator is
is 69·1555 miles.

Measurement of the Sides of Right-Angled Triangles.

315. *Problem* 1.—To find the length of any side of
a right-angled triangle, when the lengths of the other
two sides are given.

It is a property of the right-angled triangle, that the
square of the hypotenuse is equal to the sum of the
squares of the other sides.

Exercise.—Draw any right-angled triangle, and
measure the sides containing the right angle. Add
their squares, and measure the hypotenuse. If correctly done, the sum of the squares of the sides should
be the same as the square of the hypotenuse.

If the sides are 6 and 8, the hypotenuse should
be 10,   as, $6^2 + 8^2 = 10^2$;

or, $36 + 64 = 100$.

316. Hence, in a right-angled triangle, if h be the
hypotenuse, and b, p the sides containing the right
angle (base and perpendicular),

$$h^2 = b^2 + p^2;$$

Extracting the square root of each side of this equation— $\quad\quad h = \sqrt{b^2 + p^2};$ whence—

Rule 1.—To find the hypotenuse of a right-angled
triangle, extract the square root of the sum of the
squares of the sides.

317. Again— $\quad h^2 = b^2 + p^2;$

Transposing p^2, $\quad\quad h^2 - p^2 = b^2;$

Extracting the square
root— $\quad\quad \sqrt{h^2 - p^2} = b;$* whence—

Rule 2.—To find one of the sides containing the right

---

* To get the formula for finding p, we should have transposed
b^2, and thus arrived at the formula— $\sqrt{h^2 - b^2} = p$.

angle of a right-angled triangle, extract the square root of the difference of the squares of the hypotenuse and the other side.

318. *Examples and Exercises.*

1. Find the hypotenuse of a right-angled triangle, the sides being 12 feet and 9 feet.

By the formula for Rule 1—

$$h = \sqrt{12^2 + 9^2}.$$
$$12^2 = 144,$$
$$9^2 = 81,$$
$$\overline{12^2 + 9^2} = \overline{225,}$$
$$\sqrt{225} = 15,$$

the length in feet of the hypotenuse required.

2. Find the perpendicular of a right-angled triangle, the base being 21 feet, the hypotenuse 29 feet.

By the formula for Rule 2—

$$p = \sqrt{29^2 - 21^2},$$
$$29^2 = 841,$$
$$21^2 = 441,$$
$$\overline{29^2 - 21^2} = \overline{400,}$$
$$\sqrt{400} = 20,$$

the length in feet of the pendicular required.*

3. The hypotenuse of a right-angled triangle is 91 feet, and the base is 84 feet. Find the perpendicular. *Ans.*—35 feet.

4. What length of rope would reach from a window 42 feet above the ground, to a point 40 feet directly out from the bottom of the wall below the window? *Ans.*—58 feet.

---

* There is another method, sometimes convenient, for finding the difference of the squares of two numbers—*take the product of their sum and difference.*
In the example just given,—
$$29 + 21 = 50; \ 29 - 21 = 8; \ 50 \times 8 = 400.$$
Thus, $29^2 - 21^2 = (29 + 21) \times (29 - 21) = 400.$

5. The side of a square is 5 yards ; find the diagonal.
Ans.—7·071 + yards, or 7 yards, 0 feet, 2½ + inches.*

6. The hypotenuse of a right-angled triangle is 21 yards 2 feet, and the base is 18 yards 2 feet; what is the perpendicular?
Ans.—11 yards.

7. The diagonal of a square is 26 feet ; what is the length of the side?
Ans.—18·384 + feet.

8. The perpendicular from the vertex of a triangle on the base is 15 feet; the segments into which it divides the base are 8 feet and 20 feet; find the lengths of the sides.
Ans.—17 feet and 25 feet.

9. Find what must be the length of a ladder to reach to the top of a wall 48 feet high, the foot of the ladder being set at 14 feet from the bottom of the wall.
Ans.—50 feet.

10. A cord, 85 feet long, reaches from one bank of a river to the top of a tower on the opposite side close to the water, the level of which is 51 feet below the top of the tower; what is the breadth of the river?
Ans.—68 feet.

11. Find the length of the base of an isosceles triangle, each of the equal sides being 34 feet, and the perpendicular from the vertex on the base (which bisects the base) being 30 feet.
Ans.—32 feet.

12. The sides of a triangle are 29 feet and 35 feet; the perpendicular from the contained angle to the opposite side is 21 feet; what are the distances of the perpendiculars from the ends of the base?
Ans.—20 and 28 feet.

---

* The sign + after an answer means—*and a little more.*

13. Find the hypotenuse of a right-angled triangle, the sides being 85 and 132 yards.

Ans.—157 yards.

14. Find the base of a right-angled triangle, the hypotenuse being 185 feet, and the perpendicular 104 feet.

Ans.—153 feet.

15. Find the hypotenuse of a right-angled triangle, the base being 11 feet 6 inches, the perpendicular 43 feet 4 inches.

Ans.—44 feet, 10 inches.

MENSURATION OF SURFACES.

319. The extent of any surface is called its AREA, and this is usually expressed in *squares* of the measure of length in which the length and breadth of the surface are given—as, *square inches*, if the length and breadth are expressed in *inches; square feet*, if these are expressed in *feet*, and so on.

A square foot means the plane rectilineal figure called a *square*, and having each side *one foot* in length, and so on of square yard, square mile, &c.*

For the word *square*, the abbreviation *sq.* will sometimes be used.

320. *Measure of Surface or Area,*
Usually called *square* measure or *land* measure.

Sq. inches.	Sq. feet.				
144 =	1 =	Sq. yards.			
1296 =	9 =	1	Sq. poles.		
39204 =	272¼ =	30¼ =	1	Roods.	
1568160 =	10890 =	1210 =	40 =	1	Acre.
6272640 =	43560 =	4840 =	160 =	4 =	1

---

* In duodecimals the *rectangle* is sometimes used to express area or extent of surface.

A *square mile* contains 640 acres ; a *square chain* contains 16 square poles or *perches*, or 10,000 square links, and it is the tenth part of an acre.

321. An *acre* contains 10 square chains, or 100,000 square links.

Hence, to bring square links to the other land measure, *acres, &c.*—

Divide them by 100,000 ; this brings them to acres. This is done, decimally, by pointing off five figures. The figures at the left of the point, if any, are acres ; those at the right of the point are decimal parts of an acre, and are brought to roods, perches, &c., by reduction, in the usual way with decimals.

322. *French Measures of Area.*

1 metre square	=	1·196033 sq. yard.
1 are	=	0·098845 rood.
1 hectare	=	2·473614 acres.
1 sq. yard	=	0·836097 metre sq.
1 sq. pole	=	25·291939 sq. metres.
1 rood	=	10·116775 ares.
1 acre	=	0·404671 hectare.

Explanation.

323. The determination of the area of the species of parallelogram called *rectangle*, is the basis of the mensuration of areas.

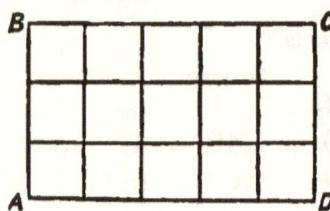

324. If the base, AD, of a rectangle, ABCD, be 5 feet in length, and the adjacent side (AB or CD) be 3 feet in length, the rectangle will contain 15 squares, each 1 foot square.

If AD be divided into 5 equal parts 1 foot each,

and lines be drawn through the points of division parallel to AB ; and if AB be divided into 3 equal parts 1 foot each, and lines be drawn through the points of division parallel to AD, it is obvious that the crossing of these lines forms a series of equal squares, each side of which is equal to one of the divisions of the base or adjacent side.

There are 5 of these squares resting on the base, and 3 rows of such squares ; altogether, 3 times 5, or 15 such squares in the rectangle.

325. Hence the rule to find the area of a rectangle— *Multiply the base by the adjacent side.* The product will be the area, expressed in squares of the unit of length used.

The rule is usually expressed, *multiply the base by the altitude*, the altitude of a rectangle being the same as the side adjacent to that taken as base. See Pars. 115, 116.

326. It is mentioned in Par. 142, that any two parallelograms on the same base, and between the same parallels, *are equal ;* so any parallelogram whatever is equal to the rectangle on *the same base* and between the same parallels. And their *altitude* is the same (115, 116), hence the rule for finding the area of a rectangle will answer for any parallelogram—*multiply the base by the altitude.*

327. A triangle is half of a parallelogram on the same base and between the same parallels. That is, if there be a triangle and a parallelogram on the same base, and if the vertex of the triangle (96) be anywhere in the opposite side of the parallelogram, or in that side produced, the triangle is half of the parallelogram. Hence the rule to find the area of a triangle—*take half the product of the base and altitude.*

MENSURATION OF RECTILINEAL FIGURES.

328. *Problem 2.*—To find the area of a parallelogram, when the base and altitude are known.

Rule.—Multiply the base by the altitude; the product will be the area, expressed in squares of the unit of measure.

If A be the area, *b* the base, and *p* the altitude (or perpendicular), then

$$A = bp.$$

329. The rule just given applies to every kind of parallelogram, whether square, rectangular, or otherwise.

If the parallelogram is a rectangle, then the two adjacent sides are base and altitude. If it is a square, then the altitude is equal to the base, and the rule is, shortly, *square the side;* that is, multiply it by itself.

330. If of the three—*area, base, altitude*—any two are known, the other may be found. From the equation—

$$A = bp,$$

dividing both sides by *p*, we have the formula—

$$\frac{A}{p} = b;$$

dividing by *b*, we get the formula—

$$\frac{A}{b} = p;$$

whence the rule for—

Problem 3.—To find the base or altitude of a parallelogram, one of these and the area being known.

Rule.—Divide the area by the other known quantity.

If the figure is a square, extract the square root of the area.

331. *Examples and Exercises.*

1. Find the area of a parallelogram, of which the base is 31 feet, the altitude 14 feet.

By the first formula above—

$$A = 31 \times 14,$$

and $31 \times 14 = 434$; whence, the area required is 434 square feet.

2. If the area of a parallelogram is 40 square yards, and the base is 16 yards, what is the altitude?

By the last-given formula—

$$p = \frac{40}{16} ;$$

and $\frac{40}{16} = 2\frac{1}{2}$; whence $2\frac{1}{2}$ yards, or 7 feet 6 inches, is the altitude required.

3. Find the area of a parallelogram, of which the base is 21 feet, the altitude 8 feet.

Ans.—$18\frac{2}{3}$ sq. yards, or 18 sq. yards 6 sq. feet.

4. Find the area of a rectangle, of which the sides are 26 inches and 13 inches.

Ans. $2\frac{25}{72}$ sq. feet, or 2 sq. feet 50 sq. inches.

5. Find the area of a square, the side of which is 18 inches.

Ans.—$2\frac{1}{4}$ sq. feet.

6. The area of a parallelogram is 100 square yards, and the base is 12 yards; what is the altitude?

Ans.—8 yards, 1 foot.

7. Find the area of a rectangular field, of which the adjacent sides are 138 and 80 yards.

Ans.—2 acres, 1 rood, 4 sq. poles, 29 sq. yards.

8. Find the total area of the four walls of a room, of which the length is 19 feet, the breadth 15 feet, and the height 12 feet; also the area of the floor or ceiling.

Ans.—The walls; $90\frac{2}{3}$ sq. yards; the floor, $31\frac{2}{3}$ sq. yards.

G

9. Find the length of the side of a square, of which the area is 1 acre.

Ans.—69·57 yards (69 yards, 1 foot, 8 + inches).

10. What is the length of a room of which the breadth is 14¼ feet, and the area of the floor 31⅔ sq. yards?

Ans.—20 feet.

11. Find the area of a field in the form of a parallelogram, one side being 123 yards, and the perpendicular on it from the opposite side, 72 yards.

Ans.—1 acre, 3 roods, 12 sq. poles or perches, 23 sq. yards.

12. Find the area of a rectangular field, of which the sides are 440 links and 311 links.

Ans.—1 acre, 1 rood, 18 sq. poles, 28 sq. yards, 5 + sq. feet.

13. What is the base of a parallelogram, of which the area is 7552 sq. yards, the altitude 64 yards.

Ans.—118 yards.

14. Find the area of a field in the form of a parallelogram, of which the base is 575 links, and the altitude 425 links.

Ans.—2 acres, 1 rood, 31 sq. poles.

15. Find the side of a square, of which the area is 500 square feet.

Ans.—22·3606 feet.

16. How much ground does the Great Pyramid cover, the base being a square, of which each side is 762 feet?

Ans.—13 acres, 1 rood, 12 sq. poles, 23 sq. yards.

17. Find the area of a parallelogram, of which the length is 12·25 chains, the altitude 8·5 chains.

Ans.—10 acres, 1 rood, 26 poles.

18. What is the area of a rectangular field, the adjacent sides of which are 13·75 chains and 9·5 chains?

Ans.—13 acres, 0 roods, 10 poles.

19. Find the extent of outer surface of a cube or cubical box, of which each edge is 5 feet 6 inches.

Ans.—20 sq. yards, 1 sq. foot, 72 sq. inches.

Note.—A cube has six square sides, equal to each other.

Problem 4.

332. To find the area of a square when the diagonal is given.

The area of a square is half the area of the square of the diagonal.

If d be the diagonal of a square—

$$A = \frac{d^2}{2}.$$

Problem 5.

333. To find the diagonal of a square when the area is known.

Extract the square root of double the area.

From the above equation, we obtain the formula—

$$d = \sqrt{2A}.$$

The diagonal of a square is the hypotenuse of a right-angled triangle, the sides of which are two sides of the square; whence the square of the diagonal is equal to the squares of the two sides (Par. 315), and as these are equal, the square of one side is equal to half the square of the diagonal.

334. *Exercises.*

1. Find the area of a square, whose diagonal is 11 feet.

Ans.—6 sq. yards, 6½ sq. feet.

2. Find the area of a square field, of which the diagonal is 121 yards.

Ans.—1 acre, 2 roods, 2 sq. poles.

3. The diagonal of a square is 15 yards. What is its area ?

Ans.—112 sq. yards, 4½ sq. feet.

4. Find the area of a square field, of which the diagonal is 524 links.

Ans.—1 acre, 1 rood, 19·66 + perches.

5. The area of a square is 34 square yards, 6½ square feet. What is the diagonal ?

Ans.—8⅓ yards.

6. Find the diagonal of a square field, of which the area is 854 square yards, 2 square feet.

Ans.—41⅓ yards.

7. Find the area of a square field, of which the diagonal is 704 links.

Ans.—2 acres, 1 rood, 36 sq. poles, 14 sq. yards, 8 + sq. feet.

8. Find the area of a square, of which the side is 35·25 chains.

Ans.—124 acres, 1 rood, 1 pole.

Problem 6.

335. To find the area of a rectangle when the diagonal and one side are known.

Rule.—Find the other side by the rule for getting one

side of a right-angled triangle when the hypotenuse and other side are known; then, base and altitude being known, proceed by Problem 2, p. 96.

If d be the diagonal, b the known side, p the other side; then,

$$p = \sqrt{d^2 - b^2},$$

and as $A = bp$, substituting in this last equation, $\sqrt{d^2 - b^2}$ for p,

$$A = b\sqrt{d^2 - b^2};$$

that is, the area of the rectangle is equal to b times the square root of the difference between the squares of d and b.

336. *Examples and Exercises.*

1. If the diagonal of a rectangle be 65 feet, and the base 63 feet, what is its area?

By the last formula—

$$A = 63 \times \sqrt{65^2 - 63^2};$$
$$A = 63 \times \sqrt{4225 - 3969};$$
$$A = 63 \times \sqrt{256};$$
$$A = 63 \times 16 = 1008. —Ans.$$

The area required is 1008 square feet, or 112 square yards; the side to be found being 16.

2. Find the area of a rectangular garden, of which the base is 200 links, the diagonal 250 links.

Ans.—1 rood, 8 sq. poles.

3. What is the area of a rectangle, of which the diagonal is 8 feet 5 inches, and a side 1 foot 8 inches?

Ans.—1 sq. yard, 4 sq. feet, 108 sq. inches.

4. Find the area of a rectangle, of which the diagonal is 65 yards, and a side 33 yards.

Ans.—1 rood, 21 sq. poles, $2\frac{3}{4}$ sq. yards.

337. The area of a parallelogram may also be found when the adjacent sides and the contained angle are known ; or, when the diagonals and the angle of their intersection are known. But *Trigonometry* is required for the solution of these problems.

Problem 7.

338. To find the area of a triangle, the base and altitude being known.

Rule.—Multiply the base by the altitude ; half of the product will be the area.

Or, the letters denoting the same quantities, as in the parallelogram, Problem 2, p. 96.

$$A = \frac{bp}{2}.$$

339. It is of no consequence at what stage of the operation the division by 2 is performed. We may reserve it to the end, as the formula indicates, or we may divide b by 2, or p by 2 before multiplying, as may appear to give the least work. It is desirable to avoid fractions, or, if possible, to reserve them to the final answer, to save multiplying or dividing them. Hence it is often well to reserve the division to the last.

340. This rule depends on the geometrical truth, that if a parallelogram and a triangle be on the same base, and between the same parallels (that is, have the same altitude), the triangle is half of the parallelogram.

Problem 8.

341. To find the base or altitude of a triangle, one of these and the area being known.

Rule.—Divide double the area by the other known quantity.

The following formulæ, deduced from the last equation, indicate how to find *base*, or *altitude*, when we know the other two of the three quantities—area, base, altitude—of a triangle:—

$$b = \frac{2A}{p}.$$

$$p = \frac{2A}{b}.$$

342. *Examples and Exercises.*

1. What is the area of a triangle, of which the base is 31 feet, the altitude 12 feet?
By the formula—

$$A = \frac{31 \times 12}{2}, \text{ and } \frac{31 \times 12}{2} = 186;$$

therefore, the area required is 186 square feet, or $20\frac{2}{3}$ square yards.

Note.—In this case, the operation is performed most easily by first dividing 12 by 2, which gives 6; multiplying 31 by this, we get the answer, 186.

2. What is the altitude of a triangle, of which the area is $8\frac{1}{3}$ square yards, the base 5 yards?
By the formula—

$$p = \frac{8\frac{1}{3} \times 2}{5}, \text{ and } \frac{8\frac{1}{3} \times 2}{5} = 3\frac{1}{3};$$

therefore, the altitude required is $3\frac{1}{3}$ yards, or 10 feet.

3. What is the area of a triangular field, of which the base is 720 links, the altitude 360 links?
Ans.—1 acre, 1 rood, 7·36 sq. poles.

4. Find the area of a triangle, of which the base is 15 feet 7 inches, the altitude 12 feet 4 inches.
Ans.—10 sq. yards, 6 sq. feet, 14 sq. inches.

5. The area of a triangular field is one acre, and its base is 121 yards; what is its altitude?
Ans.—80 yards.

6. Find the area of a triangle, of which the base is 348 feet, the altitude 198 feet.
Ans.—3 roods, 6 sq. poles, 16½ sq. yards.

7. Find the area of a triangular court, of which the base is 24 feet 6 inches, the altitude 9 feet 9 inches.
Ans.—13 sq. yards, 2 sq. feet, 63 sq. inches.

8. The base of a triangle is 58⅔ yards, the altitude 19 yards; what is its area?
Ans.—557⅓ sq. yards.

9. Find the area of a triangle, of which the base is 240 feet, the altitude 125 feet.
Ans.—1666⅔ sq. yards.

10. Find the area of a triangular field, of which the base is 1248 links, the altitude 945 links.
Ans.—5 acres, 3 roods, 23·488 perches.

11. The area of a triangular field is 3 roods, 6 sq. poles, 16½ sq. yards, and the altitude is 174 feet; what is the length of the base?
Ans.—396 feet.

12. Find the area of a triangular field, of which the base is 652 feet, the altitude 153 feet.
Ans.—1 acre, 0 roods, 23 sq. poles, 6¼ sq. yards.

Problem 9.

343. To find the area of a triangle, when the three sides are known.

Rule.—Add the three sides; from the half sum subtract each side separately; the area will be the square root of the product of the half sum and the three differences.

Let m, n, o stand for the three sides, and s for their half sum ; then

$$A = \sqrt{s\,(s-m)\,(s-n)\,(s-o)}.$$

344. *Examples and Exercises.*

1. Find the area of a triangle, of which the three sides are 26, 28, and 30 yards.
The half sum of the sides is 42.
By the formula—

$$A = \sqrt{42 \times (42-26) \times (42-28) \times (42-30)}\,;$$
$$A = \sqrt{42 \times 16 \times 14 \times 12}\,;$$
$$A = \sqrt{112986},\text{ or}$$
$$A = 336\,;$$

therefore the area of the given triangle is 336 square yards.

2. Find the area of a triangle, the three sides of which are 20, 30, and 40 feet.
Ans.—290·473 square feet.

3. Find the number of square yards in a triangle, whose sides are 30, 40, and 50 feet.
Ans.—66⅔ sq. yards.

4. Find the area of an equilateral triangle, each side of which is 25 chains.
Ans.—27·063 acres.

5. What is the area of an isosceles triangle, the base being 20 feet, and each of the equal sides 15 feet ?
Ans.—111·803 sq. feet.

6. Find the area of a triangle, whose sides are 13, 14, and 15 feet.

Ans.—84 sq. feet.

7. Find the area of a triangle, whose sides are 13, 20, and 21 feet.

Ans.—126 sq. feet.

8. Find the area of a triangular field, the sides of which are 380, 420, and 765 yards.

Ans.—9 acres, 0 roods, 38 poles.

Problem 10.

345. To find the area of a trapezoid.

Rule.—Add the two parallel sides; multiply the sum by the distance between them; half of the product will be the area.

Formula.—If s and s' denote the parallel sides, and p the distance or perpendicular between them; then—

$$A = \frac{p\,(s+s')}{2}.$$

346. *Examples and Exercises.*

1. Find the area of a trapezoid, of which the parallel sides are 28 and 18 feet, and the perpendicular between them 13 feet.

By the above formula—

$$A = \frac{13 \times (28+18)}{2};$$

$$A = \frac{13 \times 46}{2};$$

$$A = 299.$$

The area of the given trapezoid is therefore 299 sq. feet, or 33 sq. yards 2 sq. feet.

2. Find the area of a trapezoid, the parallel sides being 25 and 33 yards, the distance between them 12 yards. *Ans.*—348 sq. yards.

3. Find the area of a trapezoid, of which the parallel sides are 25 feet 6 inches and 18 feet 9 inches, and the distance between them 10 feet 5 inches. *Ans.*—230 sq. feet, 67 sq. inches.

4. Find the area of a field in the form of a trapezoid, of which the parallel sides are 750 and 1225 links, and the distance between them 1540 links. *Ans.*—15 acres, 0 roods, 33 poles.

5. What is the area of a trapezoid, of which the parallel sides are 30 chains and 46 chains, and the distance between them 60·37 chains? *Ans.*—229 acres, 1 rood, 24·66 perches.

6. Find the area of a trapezoid, of which the parallel sides are 20½ feet and 12¼ feet, and the distance between them 10¾ feet. *Ans.*—176·031 sq. feet.

Note.—This is a very useful rule. It and Problem 7 are much used in land surveying.

Problem 11.

347. To find the area of a quadrilateral or trapezium, when the four sides and a diagonal are given.
Rule.—Take the sum of the areas of the two triangles into which the diagonal divides the figure, as found by Problem 9.

Exercises.

1. Find the area of a quadrilateral ABCD, of which

the diagonal AC is 34 yards, the sides AB, BC, 19 and
24 yards, the sides AD, DC, 33 and 65 yards.
Ans.—485 + sq. yards.

2. Find the area of a quadrilateral ABCD, of which
the diagonal AC is 65 yards, the sides AB, BC, 20
and 51 yards, and the sides AD, DC, 28 and 89
yards.
Ans.—954 sq. yards.

3. Find the area of the quadrilateral ABCD, the
diagonal AC being 473 feet, the sides AB, BC, 236 and
427 feet, the sides AD, DC, 392 and 348 feet.
Ans.—117,262 + sq. feet.

Problem 12.

348. To find the area of a quadrilateral, when a diagonal and the perpendiculars on it from the opposite
angles are known.

Rule.—The area is half the product of the diagonal
and the sum of the perpendiculars upon it from the
opposite angles.

Formula.—If the diagonal be d, and the perpendiculars on it p, p', then—

$$A = \frac{d\,(p + p')}{2}.$$

Note.—The area of the figure is the sum of the areas
of the two triangles into which the diagonal divides it;
that is—

$$A = \frac{d \times p}{2} + \frac{d \times p'}{2}.$$

By adding the numerators, according to the rule for
the addition of fractions having the same denominator,

$$A = \frac{(d \times p) + (d \times p')}{2};$$

and this, as explained under "Co-efficients," Par. 273, may be simplified into—

$$A = \frac{d\,(p+p')}{2}.$$

349. *Examples and Exercises.*

1. Find the area of a trapezium, of which the diagonal is 48 feet, and the perpendiculars on it from the opposite angles 13 and 21 feet.
By the formula—

$$A = \frac{48 \times (13+21)}{2};$$

$$A = \frac{48 \times 34}{2} = 24 \times 34 = 816.$$

The answer is 816 square feet.

2. What is the area of a trapezium, of which the diagonal is 20 feet, and the perpendiculars on it from the opposite angles 4·2 and 3·8 feet?
Ans.—80 square feet.

3. Find the area of a trapezium, of which the diagonal is 84 feet, and the perpendiculars on it from the opposite angles 28 and 21 feet.
Ans.—2058 square feet.

4. Find the area of a trapezium, of which the diagonal is 65 feet, and the perpendiculars on it from the opposite angles 28 and $33\frac{1}{2}$ feet.
Ans.—222·083 square yards.

5. Find the area of a field in the form of a trapezium, the diagonal being 556 links, and the perpendiculars on it from the opposite angles 264 and 235 links.
Ans.—1·38722 acre.

6. Find the area of a four-sided field, of which the diagonal is 4·75 chains, and the perpendiculars on it from the opposite angles 2·25 chains and 3·6 chains. *Ans.*—1 acre, 1 rood, 22 poles.

Problem 13.

350. To find the area of any irregular polygon.

Rule.—By diagonals, divide the figure into triangles or quadrilaterals, or both, as may appear most convenient; find the areas of these by previous rules; the sum of these areas will be the area of the whole.

In doing this, to shorten the operation, it is desirable to work as much as possible by perpendiculars. These give the easy cases of—

Triangle, with known base and altitude;

Trapezium, with known diagonal and perpendiculars on it from the opposite angles;

Trapezoid, with known parallel sides (two perpendiculars on a side) and distance between them.

351. *Exercises.*

1. In the five-sided figure ABCDE, let the diagonal AD be 100 feet, and let there be perpendiculars on it from the angles B, C, and E—namely, B*m*, C*n*, E*o*. Let B*m* be 30 feet, meeting AD at *m*, 20 feet from A; C*n* 20 feet, at *n*, 70 from A; E*o* 10 feet, at *o*, 40 feet from A. What is the area of the figure ABCDE? *Ans.*—2350 square feet.

Note 1.—The learner should construct the figure carefully. He will find it form a triangle ADE on one side of AD; on the other side, a trapezoid between two triangles, each of which can be found by previous rules.

Note 2.—Trouble will be saved by reserving the division by 2 to the last, after the various products have been added ; then halving their sum.

2. Find the area of a field such as the preceding :— AD, 987 links ; B*m*, 97 links, 326 links from A ; E*o*, 354 links, at 543 from A ; C*n*, 158 links, 749 links from A.
Ans.—263,244 + square links.

3. Find the area of the six-sided figure ABCDEF ; diagonal AD being 30·15 feet; B*m*, 10·56, at 8·26 from A ; C*n*, 12·24, at 20·01 from A ; F*o*, 8·56, at 4·54 from A ; E*p*, 9·26, at 26·22 from A.
Ans.—470·4 + square feet.

THE REGULAR POLYGON.

352. A *Regular Polygon* is a rectilineal figure of more than four equal sides.

353. The *Centre* of a regular polygon is a point within it equidistant from the angular points. It is also equidistant from the sides.

354. The *Perimeter* of a figure is the whole length of its surrounding line or lines ; that is, in a rectilineal figure, the sum of the sides ; if the sides are equal, as in a regular polygon, the perimeter is equal to the product of one side by the number of them.

355. In a regular polygon, if perpendiculars be drawn inwards from the middle points of the sides, they will meet in one point, and be equal in length.

That point is the centre of the polygon.

The perpendicular is the radius of the inscribed circle ; and the distance from the centre to one of the angular points of the polygon is the radius of the circumscribed circle.

356. The angles of a regular polygon are equal. They increase in magnitude the greater the number of sides. See the fourth column of the table in page 113.

357. The centre is the point of intersection of the lines bisecting any two adjacent angles of the polygon.

358. The perpendicular, the length of the side being 1, is shown in the second column of the table, p. 113. It also increases as the sides are more numerous. To find the perpendicular from the centre in any polygon, the side being given, multiply the side by the number in the column of perpendiculars opposite the name of the kind of polygon given.

359. Regular polygons are named according to the number of sides :—

A Pentagon has five sides.
A Hexagon has six sides.
A Heptagon has seven sides.
An Octagon has eight sides.
A Nonagon has nine sides.
A Decagon has ten sides.
An Undecagon has eleven sides.
A Dodecagon has twelve sides.

Problem 14.

360. To find the area of a regular polygon, the side and the perpendicular on it from the centre being known.

Rule 1.—Take half the product of the perimeter by the perpendicular from the centre on a side.

Formula.—Let s be the length of a side, n the number of sides, and p the perpendicular from the centre on any side ; then, sn is the perimeter, and

$$A = \frac{snp}{2}.$$

From this equation we may extract formulæ for s and p—

$$s = \frac{2A}{np}; \quad p = \frac{2A}{ns}.$$

361. If lines be drawn from the centre to the angular points, they will form a series of equal triangles. By Prob. 7, the area of each will be equal to half the product of s the base (side of the polygon) by p the altitude $\left(\frac{sp}{2}\right)$. This, multiplied by n, the number of sides, gives the area of the whole figure.

362. *Rule 2.*—Multiply the square of the side by the number opposite the name of the polygon in the column of areas in the following table :—

Name.	Perpendicular (side 1).	Area (side 1).	Angle of the Polygon.
Equilateral triangle } ...	0·28867	0·43301	60°
Square.	0·5	1·000	90°
Pentagon.........	0·68819	1·72047	108°
Hexagon	0·86602	2·59807	120°
Heptagon.........	1·03826	3·63391	128$\frac{4}{7}$°
Octagon	1·20710	4·82842	135°
Nonagon.........	1·37373	6·18182	140°
Decagon	1·53884	7·69420	144°
Undecagon	1·70284	9·36564	147$\frac{3}{11}$°
Dodecagon	1·86602	11·19615	150°

363. *Note.*—The central angle of a regular polygon may always be found by dividing 360° by the number of sides, $= \frac{360°}{n}$.

Formula— $A = s^2 a$,

a being the area of a regular polygon of which the side is 1, as given in the third column of the Table.

364. *Exercises.*

1. Find the area of a regular hexagon, of which the side is 20 feet, and the perpendicular 17·3204 feet.
Ans.—115 sq. yards, 4 + sq. feet.

2. What is the area of a regular pentagon, of which the side is 25 feet, the perpendicular 17·2047 feet ?
Ans.—119 sq. yards, 4 + sq. feet.

3. Find the area of a regular decagon, of which the side is 7¼ feet.
Ans.—44 sq. yards, 8·4 + sq. feet.

4. Find the area of an equilateral triangle, of which the side is 20 feet.
Ans.—19 sq. yards, 2·205 sq. feet.

5. What is the area of a regular heptagon, of which the side is 237 links ?
Ans.—2 acres, 6 sq. poles, 17 + sq. yards.

6. Find the area of a regular octagon, of which the side is 20 feet.
Ans.—214 sq. yards, 5·36 + sq. feet.

7. What is the area of an equilateral triangle, the side of which is 25 feet ?
Ans.—30 sq. yards ·6 + sq. feet.

8. Find the area of a regular pentagon, of which the side is 200 links.
Ans.—2 roods, 30 poles, 3 + sq. yards.

THE CIRCLE.

365. The basis of the measurement of the circle and its parts is the relation of the circumference to the diameter.

366. By methods which are explained in more advanced works, it is ascertained that—

The circumference of a circle is $3\frac{1}{7}$ times the length of the diameter; or, otherwise expressed, $\frac{22}{7}$ times the diameter. The fraction $\frac{355}{113}$ expresses the relation still more nearly.

367. As a closer approximation, the circumference of a circle may be stated as $3\cdot14159+$ times the diameter. The number $3\cdot1416$ is generally adopted, being sufficiently correct for all ordinary purposes; and it is usual to express this number by the Greek letter π (p).

$$\pi = 3\cdot1416.$$

In the following formulæ, let C be the circumference, d the diameter, r the radius.

Note.—It is manifest from Problem 62, p. 65, that a hexagon inscribed in a circle is six times the length of the radius of the circle, or three times the diameter, which is double the radius; and it will be obvious from inspection, that the circle is a little longer than the perimeter of the hexagon—that is, a little more than three times the diameter.

Problem 15.

368. To find the circumference of a circle, the diameter or the radius being known.

Rule.—Multiply the diameter or double the radius by π. $\left(\text{Or by } \dfrac{22}{7}; \text{ or by } \dfrac{355}{113}\right).$

Formula— $C = d\pi.$

$$\left(\text{Or, } C = d \times \frac{22}{7}; \text{ or } = d \times \frac{355}{113}\right).$$

When the radius is the given quantity it must be doubled, whence the following formulæ—

$$C = 2r\pi; \left(\text{or, } = 2r \times \frac{22}{7}; \text{ or, } = 2r \times \frac{355}{113}\right).$$

Note.—The radius, multiplied by 3·1416, gives the half-circumference—*i.e.*, an arc of 180°; whence, if the radius be 1, the half-circumference is 3·1416.

Problem 16.

369. To find the diameter or the radius, the circumference being known.

Rule.—For the diameter divide the circumference by π, for the radius divide the circumference by 2π.

From the above equations the formula for the diameter or for the radius is obtained—

$$d = \frac{C}{\pi}; \quad r = \frac{C}{2\pi}.$$

Instead of dividing by π, we may multiply by its reciprocal, ·3183.*

370. *Exercises.*

1. What is the circumference of a circle of which the diameter is 17 feet?
Ans. 53·4072 feet.

---

* The number ·3183 is the reciprocal of 3·1416—that is, 1 divided by 3·1416. $\dfrac{1}{3\cdot1416} = \cdot3183.$

2. Find the circumference of a circle of which the radius is 3½ yards.

Ans.—21 yards, 2 feet, 11 + inches.

3. Find the length of a meridian circle (the earth's circumference taken through the poles), supposing the earth to be perfectly round, and 7912 miles in diameter.

Ans.—24,856 miles.

4. What is the length of the equator, supposing the earth's diameter there to be 7925½ miles?

Ans.—24,898 miles.

5. Find the diameter of a circle of which the circumference is 75 feet.

Ans.—23 feet, 10 + inches.

6. Find the radius of a circle of which the circumference is 50 yards.

Ans.—7 yards, 2 feet, 10 + inches.

7. What is the diameter of the moon, supposing that she is perfectly round, and 6785·856 miles in circumference?

Ans.—2160 miles.

8. What is the radius of a circle the circumference of which is 314·16 yards?

Ans.—50 yards.

9. The diameter of a circle is 1024 feet; what is the circumference?

Ans.—4 furlongs, 34 poles, 5 + yards.

10. The circumference of a circle is 27 yards, 1 foot, 3 inches; what is the radius?

Ans.—4 yards, 1 foot, 1 + inch.

Problem 17.

371. To find the area of a circle, the diameter being known.

Rule.—Multiply the square of the diameter by ·7854.

Formula— $A = d^2 \times ·7854.$

Note 1.—This number, ·7854, is one-fourth of 3·1416, and expresses the area of a circle whose diameter is 1— 1 being also the square of the diameter. That is, if the diameter is 1 foot in length, the area is ·7854 of 1 square foot; or, as it may be expressed roughly, a little more than *three-fourths*.

Note 2.—It is sometimes convenient to use the half-diameter or radius. As the square of half a line is one-fourth of the square of the whole line (207), so $r^2 = \dfrac{d^2}{4}$. Hence the rule—

$$A = r^2 \times 3·1416,$$

the latter number being four times ·7854.

Problem 18.

372. To find the diameter of a circle, the area being known.

Rule.—Divide the area by ·7854, and extract the square root of the quotient.

Formula— $d = \sqrt{\dfrac{A}{·7854}}$

373. *Exercises.*

1. Find the area of a circle, the diameter of which is 4 yards.

$$A = 4^2 \times ·7854.$$
$$A = 16 \times ·7854.$$
$$A = 12·5664.—Ans.$$

The answer expresses square yards, and amounts to 12 sq. yards, 5 sq. feet, 14 + sq. inches.

2. Find the area of a circle, the diameter of which is 18 feet.

Ans.—28 sq. yards, 2 sq. feet, 67 + sq. inches.

3. What is the area of a circular field, of which the diameter is 379 links ?

Ans.—1 acre, 0 roods, 20 poles, 15 + sq. yards.

4. Find the diameter of a circle, of which the area is 153·938 sq. feet.

Ans.—14 feet.

5. Find the diameter of a circle, of which the area is 1 acre.

Ans.—78½ yards, very nearly.

6. Find the area of a circle, of which the radius is 5 yards.

Ans.—78 sq. yards, 4 sq. feet, 123 + sq. inches.

7. Find the diameter of a circle, the area of which is equal to 1 square foot.

Ans.—1·12838 foot ; or 13·54 inches.

8. Find the area of a circle, of which the diameter is 5½ feet.

Ans.—2 sq. yards, 5 sq. feet, 109 + sq. inches.

Problem 19.

374. To find the area of a circle when the radius and the circumference are known.

Rule.—Take half the product of the radius by the circumference.

Formula—
$$A = \frac{rC}{2}.$$

Note 1.—This rule may be observed to be similar to the first rule for finding the area of a regular polygon, as

explained in Par. 361 $\left(A = \dfrac{snp}{2} \right)$. For, a circle may
be considered as a kind of regular polygon having a very
great number of sides, the sum of which, or perimeter,
corresponds to the circumference of the circle ($C = sn$).
The radius is the perpendicular from the centre on the
side, and the area may be considered as made up of a
great number of triangles with equal bases and perpendiculars ; the bases being very short.

Note 2.—If the diameter be taken, the divisor must
be doubled, giving—

$$A = \frac{Cd}{4}.$$

Note 3.—As before observed, the division by 2, or 4,
may be performed first, whenever it is thought this
would shorten the operation.

375. *Exercises.*

1. Find the area of a circle, of which the radius is $3\frac{1}{2}$
yards, the circumference 22 yards.
Ans.—$38\frac{1}{2}$ sq. yards.

2. Find the area of a circle, of which the radius is $2\frac{1}{2}$
yards, the circumference 15·708 yards.
Ans.—19 sq. yards, 5 sq. feet, 102 + sq. inches.

3. Find the area of a circle, of which the radius is
75 yards, the circumference 471·24 yards.
Ans.—3 acres, 2 roods, 24 poles, 5 + sq. yards.

4. What is the area of a circle, of which the diameter
is 226 links, the circumference 710 links?
Ans.—1 rood, 24 poles, 5 + sq. yards.

5. Find the area of a circle, of which the diameter is
60 feet, the circumference 188·496 feet.
Ans.—314 sq. yards, 1·44 sq. foot.

6. Find the area of a circular field, of which the diameter is 1000 links, and the circumference 3141·59* links.

Ans.—7 acres, 3 roods, 12·6 + poles.

Problem 20.

376. To find the area of a circle when the circumference is known.

Rule 1.—Divide the square of half the circumference by 3·1416.

Formula— $A = \left(\dfrac{C}{2}\right)^2 \div 3\cdot1416.$

Rule 2.—Multiply the square of the circumference by ·07958.

Formula— $A = C^2 \times \cdot07958.$

Note.—As the square of a line is 4 times the square of half the line, C^2 is 4 times $\left(\dfrac{C}{2}\right)^2$; and for the latter we may substitute C^2, in the formula for Rule 1, if we increase the divisor proportionately; whence we get the rule—

$$A = C^2 \div (3\cdot1416 \times 4).$$

The number ·07958 is the reciprocal of $3\cdot1416 \times 4$; and instead of *dividing* C^2 by the latter, we may *multiply* by its reciprocal.

377. *Exercises.*

1. What is the area of a circle, of which the circumference is 11 feet ?

Ans.—1 sq. yard, 90 + sq. inches.

---

2. Find the area of a circle, of which the circumference is 10¾ yards.

Ans.—9 sq. yards, 1·7 + sq. foot.

3. Find the area of a circle, the circumference of which is 157·08 yards.

Ans.—1963·5 sq. yards.

4. Find the area of a circle, of which the circumference is 376·992 miles.

Ans.—11309·76 sq. miles.

Problem 21.

378. To find the length of an arc of a circle, the radius and the number of degrees in the arc being known.

Rule 1.—Multiply the radius by the number of the degrees in the arc, and by 3·1416, and divide by 180.

If n be the number of degrees in the arc, then—

$$\text{Length of arc } = \frac{rn\pi}{180}.$$

Rule 2.—Multiply the radius by the number of degrees in the arc and by ·017453—the number which expresses the length of an arc of one degree when the radius is 1.

$$\text{Length of arc } = rn \times ·017453.$$

Note 1.—Rule 1 depends on this: the radius multiplied by 3·1416 gives the half circumference, or an arc of 180°; this divided by 180 gives the length of 1 degree; which, multipled by the number of degrees in any given arc, gives its length.

Note 2.—If, in working this rule, the degrees in the arc are reduced to minutes or seconds, the divisor, 180, must be reduced to the same denomination.

379. *Exercises.*

1. What is the length of an arc of 16°, the radius of its circle being 14 inches?
Ans.—3·9 + inches.

2. What is the length of an arc of 30°, the radius being 25 feet?
Ans.—13 feet, 1·08 inch.

3. Find the length of an arc of 45°, the radius being 6 yards.
Ans.—4 yards, 2 feet, 1 + inch.

4. Find the length of an arc of 57°, the radius being 38 feet.
Ans.—37 feet, 9 + inches.

5. Find the length of an arc of 120° 40′, the radius being 50 yards.
Ans.—105 yards, 0 feet, 10 + inches.

Problem 22.

380. To find the area of a sector of a circle, the radius and length of the arc being known.
Rule.—Take half the product of the radius by the length of the arc of the sector,

$$A = \frac{Arc \times r}{2}.$$

381. *Exercises.*

1. The length of an arc of a sector is 24 feet, and the radius of the circle is 15 feet; what is the area of the sector?
Ans.—20 sq. yards.

2. Find the area of a sector, whose arc is 17 feet, 3 inches, and the diameter of the circle 44 feet. *Ans.*—21 sq. yards, ·75 sq. foot.

3. Find the area of a sector, the arc (or angle) of which is one of 30°, the radius 25 yards. *Note.*—First find the length of the arc by the last problem. *Ans.*—163 sq. yards, 5 + sq. feet.

PRINTED BY BALLANTYNE AND COMPANY
EDINBURGH AND LONDON